RICHARD'S CASTLE

RICHARD'S CASTLE

Susan Coon

BLACKIE CHILDREN'S BOOKS

BLACKIE CHILDREN'S BOOKS
Published by the Penguin Group
Penguin Books Ltd, 27 Wrights Lane, London W8 5TZ, England
Penguin Books USA Inc., 375 Hudson Street, New York, New York 10014, USA
Penguin Books Australia Ltd, Ringwood, Victoria, Australia
Penguin Books Canada Ltd, 10 Alcorn Avenue, Toronto, Ontario, Canada M4V 3B2
Penguin Books (NZ) Ltd, 182–190 Wairau Road, Auckland 10, New Zealand

Penguin Books Ltd, Registered Offices: Harmondsworth, Middlesex, England

First published 1992
1 3 5 7 9 10 8 6 4 2
First edition

Text copyright © Susan Coon, 1992

The moral right of the author has been asserted

Typeset by DatIX International Limited, Bungay, Suffolk
Set in Monophoto Baskerville
Printed in England by Clays Ltd, St Ives plc

A CIP catalogue record for this book is available from the British Library

ISBN 0-216-94029-X

I

'You'll love Greenwalls Cottage, Richard,' Fay
had told me for the trillionth time that morning as
she climbed into the back of the car beside me and
pulled off her trainers. 'We always go there. It's
got its own beach, and brilliant rock pools and
this magic castle and every year there's a raft race.
And you'll meet Jack and Josie. We always have
terrific fun. You'll love it.'

That was the trouble with being adopted. Everyone else, even your *little* sister, already knew everything. Fay didn't understand that I wanted to
discover these things for myself, but I could just
see the hurt look that would appear on her podgy
face if I ever said anything. So I never did. She
meant well. Didn't they all?

But it was at this point, seven or eight hours
into the journey, that I had my Idea. I *would*
discover these places for myself. I wouldn't wait to
be shown them – even if it meant sneaking out of
the house at 3 a.m. Brill. I felt really good once
I'd had my Idea.

I suppose there is something comforting about a
family who always give you breakfast in bed on
your birthday, who always do the weekly shopping

on Friday evening and who always go to Green-walls Cottage for their holidays. Life with the Kings is certainly more reliable than the chaotic version of daily life with my real mother – no, my old mother, who sometimes bothered about birthdays but tended to have breakfast in bed anyway, who sometimes had enough food in the house but often sent me to the chip shop for dinner at night – and once for breakfast – and who could never afford a holiday except the year she had a boyfriend and they went to Blackpool and lost me on the beach. Deliberately.

So I don't mind the reliability of birthdays and meals. It's just that word 'always' that makes me feel sort of trapped.

Not long after Idea time, Dad said, 'Nearly there,' and turned the car slowly into a bumpy driveway.

I leant forward to see better and Fay slumped behind my back. You could just make out a white metal fence and clumps of giant rhododendrons. Ahead, a porch light shone at the entrance to a whitewashed cottage.

As Dad finally brought the car to a stop beside Uncle Steve's blue Volvo Estate, curtains flicked at the window and I felt the chicken and chips from the Little Chef come to life in my stomach. Jack was my only male cousin, you see, and I'd been imagining all the fun we'd have together, exploring the pools and the castle, building rafts, telling jokes on the beach, all that stuff.

I have this mantra. It's a survival technique I learnt. You sort of hypnotize yourself with it. 'It doesn't matter, nothing matters. It doesn't matter, nothing matters.' It took about six goes this time before I got myself numb.

'What a journey!' exclaimed Mum, washing her face with her hands to wake herself up. She un-clipped the seat belt and opened the door. 'Wake up, everyone. We're here.'

Meanwhile, members of the McPherson family were spilling out of the house. Mum and Auntie Chris – they were so alike, their voices and manner-isms and hair-styles – had fallen into each other's arms.

'Such a journey!'

'Where've you been?'

'First the roadworks on the M6 . . .'

'We were getting worried.'

'Then a puncture on the A75.'

'Never mind. I'll get the kettle on.'

'Such a nuisance the cottage not being on the phone.'

'I've got dinner ready.'

'Oh, I knew you would, Chris. But everyone was so hungry we had to stop and eat.'

'Oh well, we've got enough men here now to polish off the leftovers later,' Auntie Chris laughed. She said something in Mum's ear.

Mum glanced at me still in the car and smiled. 'He'll come in his own time. That's best,' she said.

I nudged Fay. Someone was shrieking her name.

She straightened herself with a yawn, a stretch and a groan and sat blinking, still half asleep. She always sleeps in the car and she always takes off her trainers and I always have to find them. Always, always. Still, that's one always that wasn't here before me, I suppose.

'Uncle Steve,' she mumbled.

I recited, 'Manager of a jam factory, plays golf, fun.'

'Auntie Chris.'

'Mum's older sister, an accountant, bossy.'

'Josie.'

'Our cousin, your age, brilliant at gymnastics.'

'Jack.'

'Our cousin, two years older than me, brilliant at —'

Because it mattered, I'd forgotten. But Fay was stumbling out of the car. Uncle Steve, who was tall and slim and dark like Dad hoisted her up for a boisterous hug and kiss then let her down. He didn't say, 'My what a big girl,' or anything soft like that, which was a good sign and nice of him, as Fay was getting worried about her weight.

I shut the door and hovered as Fay made her way to the source of the shrieking. It (Josie) was tall and slim, poor Fay, dressed in pyjamas and jumping up and down. They too linked arms and disappeared into the house like another pair entering the ark.

I was just wondering where Noah was and feeling a bit anxious that *my* partner hadn't appeared when Uncle Steve held out his hand.

'Hi, Richard. Good to meet you at last. Sorry you've had a rotten journey. Welcome to Greenwalls Cottage.'

Before I could reply I saw, looming over his shoulder, my cousin Jack. He had dark curly hair and blue, self-confident eyes. He wore a Dark Poppies T-shirt with tour dates down the back and those black denims that get you into nightclubs on telly ads. Not only was he two years older than me, he was two feet taller. One look at the bored expression on his spotty face told me it wasn't going to work.

It doesn't matter, nothing matters.

'Hi, Uncle Martin. Hi, cuz,' he said, without looking either of us in the eye.

'Hi,' I said, not being one to give up easily. Cuz!

'Why is unloading the car always left to the men?' he drawled.

Mr Cool helped himself to four bags, admittedly the smaller ones that were crammed on the top, but I couldn't help feeling he was making a point.

I managed two bags without tripping, in spite of the fact that I could barely keep them off the ground and my arms felt as though they were getting long enough for a gorilla. Two to me, four to him, I thought. Swine.

The cottage was beautifully furnished. I saw that I would have to be careful not to spill things. So I deliberately put the mug of cocoa on the coffee table before taking another piece of fruit cake from Auntie Chris. I said very little and kept out of everyone's way, another survival technique.

Right now, my task was to recognize allies. Fay and Josie were giggling together on the floor, brushing and plaiting Fay's blond hair. Josie was brilliant at gymnastics. She looked sort of bendy, the way she lowered herself to the floor and crossed her legs, making it look quite natural. As long as she didn't see me as a rival, I thought I'd be OK there.

Auntie Chris sat on the sofa beside Mum, bare feet tucked under her, chattering and giggling as much as Josie and Fay. She wore a T-shirt that said, 'Give me TIME,' and showed a clock face with no hands. She seemed nervous.

Uncle Steve and Dad were already on to night-caps and seemed to be enjoying their reunion too because every so often a burst of laughter came from their sofa. Uncle Steve's eyes wrinkled at the sides as though he laughed a lot. He seemed an easy person to like. Twice he'd winked at me in a friendly but not pushy way.

The cake came round again. Everyone – especially Mr Cool, I thought – was ignoring me except when they had to offer me food and drink. Giving me time, Mum called it. She tends to make out that I'm shy and nervous of new people but I'm not. I'm just careful.

Fay was obviously torn between Josie, who was chattering away as though she hadn't been allowed to talk for days and Mr Cool, who had flopped nonchalantly (he thought) on an arm-chair, with one long leg hooked over the arm. What a poser. I couldn't help it. I didn't like him.

It doesn't matter. Nothing matters.

Fay walked over and sat herself at Mr Cool's foot.

'What d'you want to do tomorrow?' she enquired. 'I like your T-shirt.'

Mr Cool smiled down at her condescendingly, then gave a nonchalant shrug.

'Show Richard round, I s'pose.' He walked his eyes along the floor and up my jeans and plain blue T-shirt. 'You like fishing?'

Not if you do it, I thought. I shrugged.

'Never done it?'

I shook my head.

'I got a new rod,' he announced in his bored voice. 'Looking forward to trying it out. Number one place is the estuary.'

'There are the rock pools,' suggested Josie. She smiled encouragingly at me but I forgot to smile back. Sometimes I forget people can see me.

'Or the castle,' added Fay.

'Yeah. I'll show you everything,' Mr Cool drawled.

'Thanks,' I said. But no thanks. I don't need you to show me anything, you creep.

'Oh, Richard,' Auntie Chris was saying, 'Jack always sleeps in the wee room through there.' She waved vaguely out of the sitting-room. 'So I thought you'd probably like to sleep there too.

But if you prefer your own room, it's no bother to move the bed into the study. It's actually not a bed,' she turned apologetically to Mum. 'It's just a mattress and sleeping bag, but it's a good mattress. He should be quite comfortable.'

'I told you, Mum. I'll have it,' drawled Mr Cool, earning himself a point. That made it 5–2.

'It doesn't matter,' I insisted. After four different foster homes and families and schools, you soon learn that things like that really *don't* matter.

'I'll show you, Richard,' offered Fay, struggling to her feet, while Josie seemed to grow out of the floor in one smooth movement.

'I'm sure he'll find it when he wants,' Auntie Chris said.

So, I thought, I'm not to be sent to bed like a kid. I suppose that's because they want me to be old enough for Mr Cool. Hmm. Could have its advantages.

'I'll just show him, though. Of course he doesn't have to go to bed,' Fay said, catching on.

'Come on then,' I said. Now you can all talk about me. Get it over with.

'This is Jack's room through here,' Fay said, leading me into the hall. 'We sleep upstairs,' she said, indicating a wide staircase with a curving wooden banister. 'That's the dining-room, behind the study, kitchen, downstairs loo, and here we are.'

It was a pretty average room, all white, with a big wardrobe and chest of drawers and one bed.

On the floor was the mattress we were fighting over and a brown and yellow flowery sleeping bag.

I looked at the books on the chest of drawers, Isaac Asimov, Frank Herbert, Anne McCaffrey.

'Jack's into science fiction,' Fay said, pushing past me to let Josie in.

I wished he really was.

'What d'you think of him? Pretty cool, isn't he?'

'Yeah.' So cool he's frozen.

'Right. G'night then.'

She put her arm round my neck and pulled me down to plant a kiss on my cheek. Like I said, she means well.

Then Josie slid forwards. She looked at Fay uncertainly, her cheeks flushed and said, 'Can I ask you something, Richard?'

'Yeah.'

'Are you an orphan or what? Is that why Auntie Anne and Uncle Martin adopted you?'

No one had ever come out with it like that. It sort of caught me unawares and I said, 'Uhuh.'

'How did it happen? Car crash or something?'

'Uhuh.'

Josie made one of those sympathetic faces then kissed me.

'I'm sorry,' she said. 'You must miss them some-times, even though you've got a new family.'

I ignored Fay's open-mouthed silence.

The girls skipped upstairs and I threw myself down on the mattress cursing.

Rats! Rats! Triple Rats! Why did I have to lie?

I'm no good at entrances. If I'd gone back then, I knew the conversation would suddenly have stopped. Everyone would have tried to smile at me without looking right at me and Auntie Chris would probably have been all watery-eyed. Unless, of course, as usually happened, Mum had briefed them first by phone. Still, there was always the 'how's he getting along?' bit to go through. So I left them to it.

I don't sleep in cars and somehow doing nothing all day makes me tired so I just went to bed. Ever so faintly, I could hear laughter in the living-room.

It wasn't long before Mr Cool came through.

'Oh, you're here! Hey,' he kicked the mattress, 'I said I'd have it, cuz.'

'I'm OK.'

'We'll take it in turns.'

What a fuss about nothing. Imagine fighting over a mattress. But I knew it wasn't just that, so I propped myself up on my elbows and planned to earn another point or two.

'You don't have to be nice to me, you know,' I said. 'I'm not soft.' One to me. 3–5.

Mr Cool paused with his T-shirt over his head. His lips twitched.

'Oh, but I do,' he grinned, gaining a point for exquisite timing. 'I've been told to.'

Wow! He was as straight-talking as his sister.

'Well, I'm not asking you to,' I said, recovering quickly enough to make it 4–6.

'I know,' he said, as though it was no big deal. 'So, now that's understood,' he went on smoothly, 'I'll take you fishing tomorrow morning and to the rock pools tomorrow afternoon and to the castle in the evening and that'll be my duty done.'

He picked up a towel and flung it over his spotty shoulder. I squirmed off my mattress, still in my bag, and beat at his pillow with both fists until I felt exhausted, really quite weak, as though I might faint or cry. That made me angrier still.

I don't need you to take me anywhere you big, slimy, smooth swine. I don't need anyone to take me anywhere. I never did and I don't now. 4–6 to you doesn't matter. Nothing matters. It doesn't matter, nothing matters.

Then the Idea came back to me and I wriggled down on my mattress and set the alarm on my watch for 3 a.m.

2

At 3 a.m. my alarm went off and I caught the button on the second bleep. I lay still to see whether Mr Cool had been disturbed, but the covers on the other side of the room continued to gently rise and fall. In a few minutes, my carrot vision was good enough to distinguish the shapes of the wardrobe, the chest of drawers and, most of all, Mr Cool's bed, that I must not bump.

I pushed down the sleeping bag, so there'd be no unzipping noise to wake Mr Cool, took the torch from under my pillow and crawled to the end of the mattress. Carefully feeling for the clothes I'd left neatly at the end of the bed, I scooped them in my arm, slid the torch inside one of my trainers and made sure it was secure before standing up and aiming for the door.

The worst part would be actually turning the knob. This I did very slowly and with hardly any noise.

In the bathroom, I pulled jeans and a jumper over my pyjamas and tied my trainers on to bare feet. I pushed the torch into my pocket and was about to open the door when I heard a floorboard creak in the hall. My hand froze on the handle while I listened, waiting for someone to come. Then it occurred to me that everyone who slept upstairs would use the upstairs bathroom or, if that were occupied and they had to come down here, they would switch on the light. So, whoever was coming now, stealthily, in the dark, didn't want to be discovered.

The someone was feeling his way along the wall, fumbling for a door handle, now turning it and going into the kitchen. I heard the snap of the light switch.

Fay! You little cheat! No wonder you're getting so fat.

I had already decided to go out of the back door in the kitchen as there were quiet concrete slabs and a lawn that way, while from the front door led a noisy, crunchy, gravel path. So I waited.

While I waited, I reasoned that if Fay and I did meet, she could hardly tell on me, because I'd just been going to the toilet (as long as I took off my clothes) whereas she'd been secretly stuffing. It never did any harm to have something on someone. She'd got there first, so to speak, having been born a King, whereas I had only been there for six months and the adoption hadn't been confirmed by the court yet. Things like that counted, no matter what anyone said.

Luckily for Fay, I couldn't be bothered to take off my clothes and trainers.

At last I heard her snap off the light and feel

her way through the hall and up the stairs. I waited another five minutes before considering it safe to move.

In the kitchen, I gazed round the square room, wondering where the key might be. No chance of it being still in the door? No.

At home, the key had hung on a string behind the letterbox until Mum went to a women's safety course. Then she moved it out of finger reach and you had to know that the broken coathanger lying casually amongst the sweet peas was not a weird gardening tool but a sophisticated, ingenious and perfectly legal method of breaking and entering. Well, entering.

At one of my foster homes, there had been a brass rack that said 'keys' and everyone left their car keys and bicycle padlock keys there. At another house there was a sweetie tin, which, Auntie Pip had claimed, would fool any burglar who broke in through a window and wanted to open a door to carry out the large items. At yet another house, keys, library tickets, pencils, fuses and shoelaces were kept in 'the' drawer.

I scanned the room. Beep beep beep tea caddy, no. Beep beep beep cutlery drawer, no. Beep beep beep flower pot – flower pot? Empty flower pot? I leant over the sink and lifted the flower pot. It was empty but underneath it, eureka!

Then I was tiptoeing over the grass, past the side window of the room where Mr Cool still slept. I ducked into the trees, where the shadows would hide me but a tree root or bramble tripwire sent me flying into the deepest rhododendron thicket.

I picked myself up and made my way round this thicket to the driveway and was relieved to find it so easily. I used the torch once. The driveway was just compacted mud, dry and dusty after the summer but mossy and weedy in the middle.

After a while, it crossed a stream that burbled toward the sea and on my right I could hear the stream tipping itself over some rocks and splashing down to the sea.

Soon, I vowed, I'll know as much about this place as anyone and I'll have had the fun of discovering it myself. I needn't be impressed if I don't want to be. But I *can* be impressed if I *do* want to be. That was it. No one would be there to say, 'This is the best bit,' or, 'That's nothing, come over here,' or, 'That boring castle.'

I stopped there, because suddenly the moon slid from behind a cloud and the castle I had just imagined loomed ahead of me, a huge, uneven, black silhouette, a bit eerie the way it just appeared like that. I took a few breaths then began to creep forwards, slowly, quietly, my eyes fixed on the shape of one crenellated tower. I was Robin Hood, about to rescue Marian. Then, as suddenly as it had come, it went, as another cloud covered the moon.

I blinked and swallowed and stopped again. Suddenly it occurred to me that the castle still might be occupied. Where had Fay said they used to play? I broke out in a sweat trying to remember. Rats! I couldn't be sure.

I decided that, if necessary, I could run off pretty quickly, so I risked the torch and edged up the driveway again until the bushes thinned and there was a big, open, grassy space in front of me. I shone the torch up ahead and although the beam was pretty faint, I could see enough to know the castle wasn't occupied.

Apart from that one tower it was a ruin.

The driveway curved in front of it and off to my left. There were bits of walls and heaps of rubble that suggested the building had once been square, with a tower at each corner. But I didn't fancy that rubble at night so, playing the torch from right to left, I followed a little path round the right side of the castle which I hoped would lead me to the tower.

I hadn't gone far when I thought I heard the sound of an engine. I switched off the torch and listened but decided it was the sea I could hear. Still, I didn't use the torch again because it was more exciting in the dark. I ran the fingers of my left hand along the stones, until I sensed, rather than saw, something ahead. Reaching out, I found a wooden barrier extending from the tower wall across the path and into a clump of bushes. I was sure I could hear, way, way, below, the lapping of waves. I stepped back, wondering whether to risk my carrot vision or use the torch, when suddenly there was a clattering noise and a flash as a small metallic object bounced past and tumbled below.

Something flew out of a nearby bush and flapped off in a panic. I pinned myself against the wall, my heart thudding. When nothing else happened, I decided it was safe to breathe again and peered up at the tower, but of course there was nothing to see.

I eased myself away from the wall. A pigeon cooed softly and then an owl hooted, 'Hooo?'

'Meeee,' I replied, to prove I wasn't scared.

But I raced back to the front of the building and only slowed to a walk once I was well down the driveway.

This had been a totally wasted trip. What had I gained? Did it really feel good to know there was one intact tower and a few heaps of rubble at the castle? I'd have to keep this little secret all to myself, in a corner of my mind, unseen and unappreciated by anyone else. What was the use if you couldn't show off to someone else?

Then I thought, wasn't that the point? The fact that I wouldn't have to deal with that awful feeling of being watched by Fay or Mum or Dad, all hoping I'd say, 'Wow, it's fantastic. Thank you for showing me. I'm so grateful to you for sharing your treasured place, which is of course your treasured place because you were here first.' Or something.

As the driveway turned, I glanced back over my shoulder. The moon was clear again and the tower was silhouetted against it, all jagged and angry. I shivered and began to jog, just to keep warm, and as I jogged, I realized I could do this every night. Visit the beach before I had to go there with them, or learn to fish without Mr Cool having to teach me.

But then I stopped myself. The Kings meant well. All of them, including the McPhersons. Mum with her 'protective distance' ideas, Dad with his 'treat-him-like-a-man' plan and Fay with her 'fore-warned is forearmed' whisperings. It must be difficult for them too, sometimes, not really knowing how to treat me. And it was certainly better with the Kings than it had been with Mum, after . . .

So what if Fay had done lots of things before me? It wouldn't be for much longer. Already I was catching up with my school work. I'm a quick learner, everyone says that. 'He has his wits about him.' God, you had to have to survive with my mum – I mean my old mum.

Suddenly, I heard a sound from behind, the sound of a diesel engine. I stopped and turned and saw headlights breaking through the trees, almost at the bend. I dived off the path, tripped on a bramble and pitched into a thick rhododen-dron bush. It was so thick that I actually sprang back. So I flung myself desperately underneath it and just had time to wriggle my body round to face the driveway. Then I pulled a broken twig over my face and watched.

It was a light-coloured jeep, but the brightness of the headlights made it impossible to make out more than that. The back number plate bounced around a lot. E something 3 or 8, something, something S. Had someone really been up in the tower then? Or were these sheep rustlers or poachers? Should I tell the farmer?

But how could I?

I picked myself out of the brambles and bushes, patted my pocket to check the torch and key were still there and walked the rest of the way back to the cottage, keeping to the edge of the driveway and deciding it was none of my business and I should just keep quiet as usual.

There was no sign that anyone was up and had discovered me missing. The sky was very much lighter now in the east. Dawn, it's called, but it was still dark at the back of the cottage so I moved very cautiously past Mr Cool's window. The kitchen door opened easily. I didn't forget to lock it behind me and soon I was safely in the bathroom, pulling off my jeans and sweater and toeing off my trainers. I checked over them for signs of damage but because the ground was so dry, I was still pretty clean.

I crept back to the bedroom, replaced my clothes on the end of my mattress and wriggled into the brown and yellow sleeping bag, feeling like a corpse surrounded with flowers.

Mr Cool snorted in his sleep.

I stuffed the sleeping bag in my mouth to stop myself laughing. Surely an escapade like this was worth a bonus point.

I'd done it. I'd done it. I'd done it.

And if I'd done it once, I could do it again.

3

When I wake up, I always lie still and listen until I've sussed out a few things; the time, the temperature, how hungry I am, whether anyone else is up, what sort of mood they're in, that kind of thing.

This morning I woke up with a picture of a black square on a white circle in my mind and couldn't think where it had come from. There was no sound. Mr Cool's bed was empty and I was hungry. The sun was streaming through the transparent curtains and it was ten thirty.

Ten thirty!

I washed and dressed quickly. The sound of voices in the dining-room told me where they were but, like I said, I'm not good at entrances so I went into the kitchen and rummaged for cereal. I opened the Bran Flakes, then made myself two slices of toast and opened a jar of jam. I knew it was wrong when there were probably all kinds of jars open next door but I couldn't be bothered with the moist eyes and the condescending comments.

'You're up!' cried Mum, unnecessarily, making me jump. She was balancing a tray of dirty bowls, plates and mugs.

'Oh! You're up!' exclaimed hawk-eyed Auntie Chris, following with another tray of leftovers.

I smiled pathetically since I couldn't think of an interesting but honest reply. Yes, I'm up, this is me, prod prod. Yes, it really is me, you're perfectly right.

'Did you sleep well?' asked Auntie Chris. (Today's T-shirt proclaimed her to be, 'Over the hill but not round the bend.' A matter of opinion.) 'I didn't think the mattress would be too bad,' she went on, bustling around putting things away while I hopped from one wrong place to another and she said, 'Sorry, I'm getting in your way,' which was a silly thing to say because it was the other way round. It was all part of the, 'Be nice to Richard, he's had a hard time,' bit.

'We're going to make a picnic, Richard, and take it down to the beach.' She broke off, staring into one of the cupboards. 'I could have sworn . . . Richard you weren't; I mean you didn't,' she glanced at Mum. 'Oh nothing. It doesn't matter.'

You're learning, I thought.

'Be a pet and dry would you, Richard?' Mum asked. 'I'm running out of space.'

'It's all right, I'll do it,' said Auntie Chris. 'Richard'll want to go off with Jack, won't you? Run along. He's in the garden.'

I didn't mind being asked and I didn't mind helping. But Auntie Chris had assumed I would. People were always doing that. Telling me what I wanted or didn't want. I went out and closed the door slowly so that I could listen.

'Doesn't say much, does he?'

'Never. He's really locked up.'

'I suppose a lot of things are still strange for him, poor wee soul.'

I gritted my teeth.

In the garden, Mr Cool was examining a fishing rod through his shades. Fay and Josie were dancing round him.

'Hi,' he drawled without looking up.

'Hi.'

'This is Jack's new rod. It's great, isn't it?'

'Yeah.'

I knew nothing about fishing or rods. I looked at a tray of hooks on the grass and I thought how it would hurt to get one of those barbs in your finger, or your mouth.

'Know much about it?' Mr Cool asked.

'I think it's cruel,' I replied, feeling all hot.

Fay looked at me as though I'd sprouted horns. How dare I criticize her hero! I felt my hands balling into fists.

'Cruel? You a veggie?'

'Eating's one thing. Killing for sport's another.' One to me, I thought. 6 all.

'But you don't kill them. You put them back.'

Rats! 6–7.

'All frightened and suffocating and cut and bleeding?'

'They're only fish. They don't have feelings.'

'How do you know?'

'Well . . . Why don't you come along anyway?

22

You shouldn't make up your mind till you've tried it.'

I didn't like this reasonable approach because if I didn't go along with it I'd look ignorant.

I stared at the vicious hooks.

'Will you catch something nice for my dinner, Jack?' Fay cooed at him.

'Course.'

Mr Cool blinked lazily and smiled, sopping up the admiration like a sponge but pretending not to notice it.

I wandered over to the hedge so as not to be sick. Fay followed.

'And will *you* catch something nice for my dinner, Richard?' she cooed disgustingly.

'No! You'd get fat!'

Rats! Why did I have to open my mouth! The silence, as they say, said it all. Her eyes were watering and met mine reproachfully. Her lips were pulled together in an effort not to cry. She was scared, I saw, and surprised. Hurt and fear would make her attack. I braced myself.

'You know that's not a nice thing to say.' Her voice wobbled. 'You know I'm dieting. I wasn't serious about eating two fishes. I know I'm always on at you for never saying anything but I think I'd rather you kept your opinions to yourself if that's the kind of thing you're going to say.'

I caught her arm as she turned to bounce off and saw a flicker of hope in her damp eyes. It was habit, though. I couldn't stop myself.

'Fay, I was in the bathroom when you came down last night,' I whispered.

Her eyes widened with horror and panic.

'You wouldn't!' she hissed. She pulled her arm free and jerked her shoulder as she turned her back on me without letting me say, 'Of course not.'

'Come on, Josie,' she said.

I watched them pick up their towels and leave the garden and didn't miss the narrowed eyes of Josie as she sent me a 'how could you?' look on her way past.

Mr Cool said, once they'd gone, 'You're quite right. She is fat.'

The swine!

'She dotes on you!'

'She's got a crush on me, yes, but that doesn't make her any less fat.' Satisfied that the nylon line was moving freely through the loops, he slid the rod back into its canvas case. 'Besides, *I* didn't say it to her face.'

'No, but . . .'

'Did I? Have *I* done or said anything to hurt her feelings?'

'No.'

'Well, then. You coming?'

I supposed I had to. 'Where to?'

Mr Cool strode over to the hedge and nodded. 'We don't want to go to the beach too early. The tide's out till this afternoon. See?'

Over the hedge, the shimmer of water I'd seen

24

from the house was no more than that – a silver thread along the horizon, thickening as it wove westwards towards the channel where the river met the sea.

'So you might as well come along,' Mr Cool said. 'Of course you don't have to if you don't want to. 'S up to you.'

I wondered if this was a let-off I could take without losing face. Then I applied one of my rules, one of my survival techniques, which was to learn as much as possible about every thing, every place and every one. Because you never knew . . .

'I'll come,' I said, with what I hoped was a nonchalant shrug.

The path to the fishing rock forked off the path to the beach and took us through some tall, prickly bushes. It was so overgrown that I knew I'd have missed it on my own.

Eventually, we reached the rocks that divided the beach from the river estuary. Even with the tide far out, the silver curve of the channel could be seen, and even if you couldn't have seen it you'd have known it was there by the noise of the gulls and other birds wheeling, diving and strutting around. A flashing light marked the end of the rocks.

'That's where we're going,' Mr Cool pointed. 'When the tide turns, the flatties all rush up here. You can hardly help catching them,' he said with a grin.

You can, I thought. You don't have to stick that baited hook in the water.

'Look at those oystercatchers. And the terns, there!'

They were just birds to me but I looked politely. I'd read *Jonathan Livingstone Seagull*. Of course it was fiction but . . .

I found a smooth rock and sat and waited as the tide turned and Mr Cool couldn't help catching fish, twisting the hook out of their mouths and throwing them back.

'Want a turn?'

I shook my head.

'Must be pretty boring, just watching.'

I remembered I was there to learn so I reached out and said, 'OK, I'll have a shot. Probably won't catch anything though.' Hope I don't catch anything.

But I did. I gasped at the first tug and Mr Cool was on his feet immediately.

'Let it rest,' he called. 'Pull it up a bit, give it some slack, pull it in a bit. See it? Rest. Now! Right up. That's it.'

To my disgust, I recognized a sense of triumph as the 'flattie' landed and flapped.

'It's a nice big one,' Mr Cool said. 'If we keep it for dinner, will you feel better?'

I nodded, though by now, I realized, watching as Mr Cool unhooked the fish and slid it into a net that he kept in the water, I had seen so many thrown back and swim safely away that I was beginning to share his view. A bit. Maybe the fish even enjoyed the excitement, the game, the near

26

miss, like climbing a tree and falling and getting away with just a scratch.

'Want to carry on?'

My palms were sweating. I licked my lips. Well, is it cruel or isn't it if the fish don't choose the game? I handed back the rod.

'Naw. You carry on.'

I waded round the corner, and sat out of sight on a warm smooth black fist of rock. I thought I knew what was right and what was wrong on things like cruelty and killing. I kicked my feet in the water, letting the sun heat the back of my neck and shoulders. I know I often get mixed up when I say things – like this morning – but I thought I knew what I believed in. And I didn't feel cruel.

Just tired. After last night. The sun hurt my eyes and as I let them close, suddenly I saw in my mind, the black square of the tower against the white circle of the moon.

Next thing I knew, Mr Cool was calling me. I must have dozed off because the tide was much further in and he'd caught another good-sized fish for supper.

'Look, I'd better get these back to the cottage and put them in the fridge. Dad can gut them when he gets back from golf.' He was swinging two round, sandy-coloured things with horrid, desperate mouths. 'Better take the rod up, too, for safe-keeping. Will you go on? The beach is just over those rocks.'

I nodded.

'And could you take these for me?'

He kicked at his towel and T-shirt and shorts but didn't wait for my reply. Cheek! I'd a good mind to leave them. Say I hadn't heard. Of course, Jack. Anything you say, Jack.

The beach was barricaded on either side by jagged rocks like long fingers clawing the sand. It was too small for most people to bother scrambling to, but nice for one family.

I'd hardly settled myself and told them about dinner, when Mr Cool came racing out of the bushes and leapt down a flight of steps, landing and rolling over in the sand.

'I hope that's *your* sandwiches you've covered in grit,' remarked Auntie Chris.

'That's why they're called sandwiches, I suppose. Ha ha,' said Mr Cool, looking at his watch and at the sky as if trying to remember something. 'Six thirty-five. I had it down to six twenty last summer.'

'You're just out of practice,' Auntie Chris said. 'Not that I'm encouraging you. Racing up and down that path's dangerous.'

'I know where the dangerous bits are.'

'And how long to get up?' Mum asked.

'Eleven dead it was. What about you, Richard? You a runner?' enquired Mr Cool, rolling over and propping himself on his elbows.

'A runner?'

Why did he make everything sound like a challenge?

'Yeah. You look as if you could be. Right build for a distance runner, cross country, say. Good balance. I saw you on the rocks, dancing about.'

I helped myself to a cheese and salad sandwich with a shrug. I could run. Of course I could run. Everyone can run.

'Bet you're something at cross country.'

I shook my head.

'Jack's the school champion. Runs for the county,' Josie announced, dropping her towel on the sand and flopping on to it.

'Bet you could be, too,' Mr Cool went on. He rolled on his back, shading his eyes with one hand and feeding himself with the other. I waited for him to choke. But he didn't.

No one was telling him that I had to miss extra games to catch up on English and Maths and I was grateful for that. All the same, it would be nice to be good at something. Running would do.

As if reading my mind, Mr Cool announced, 'Richard's going to try the path run.'

Josie grinned. 'You'll beat my times anyway.'

'Walk it first,' Mr Cool said, like a caring older cousin. 'There are some zigzags you need to know about. And wait till it's cooler.'

'My best's fifteen minutes five for up and eight minutes twenty-two for down,' Josie said.

I didn't know that I fancied racing up and down that path. It was a simple enough thing, only so much depended on it. Mr Cool's respect. And therefore, everyone's respect. I was losing

Fay. Not that I wanted her hanging on but I didn't like the idea of her sucking up to that arrogant swine either.

I went to scramble around the rocks on the other side of the beach, testing Mr Cool's assertion that I had good balance. It seemed to be true, which gave me hope that the rest of it might be.

I peered into a pool and watched the sun yellow the rough, sandy rock. I put my hand in the pool. The water was hot. I splashed my feet in the pool then leant back. My head landed on something uncomfortable. I moved but it was still lumpy. That was the trouble with rocks. I sat up and looked for a better spot and then I saw what my head had been hitting.

Jammed in a cleft was a metal torch. I wrestled it free and switched it on unthinkingly and only as it started flashing did I realize where I was standing.

Naturally, I looked up at the steep sandstone cliffs but I was too close to see to the top. I made my way back out on the rocks until I could see where the top of the cliffs joined into the dark geometrical shape of the castle walls and of the tower, exactly where I'd been standing last night when *something* had clattered past me.

4

'When are you going to do the path run, Richard?'
Josie asked as we climbed back up.

'Huh. When he gets the guts,' snorted Mr Cool
who was carrying all the food bags, now that they
were empty. I wasn't giving him a point for that.

'After he's walked it both ways,' he said in a
louder voice. I looked up and saw the reason for the
louder voice, or rather the reasons – the Dads –
standing at the gate. 'But I tell you what, cuz, if you
like you can come training with me this evening.'

'If you like.'

'No, if *you* like.'

Mr Cool stopped and turned and looked at me,
holding up the whole caravan.

'Make a decision for once,' he muttered.

I met his eyes but said nothing.

'Come on, Jack,' called Josie.

'There are a couple of good loops,' he said
loudly, beginning to climb again. 'We'll do the
four mile and see how you get on. Down the
driveway to the lodge, up the road to the farm-
track, up the farm-track past the farm, then back
across the fields. The six mile takes you all the
way round the farm-track to the castle and back.'

It turned out that dinner was going to be late, so Mr Cool decided we should run before eating.

'Half an hour,' Josie shouted as we set off down the rutted driveway.

'Don't listen to her,' he said. 'Take your time. It's too warm.'

Mr Cool held back, I knew, letting me set the pace. Well, I thought, I'll show you.

Of course I had no idea what four miles felt like but I was sure it wasn't much. I stretched my legs to show him I wasn't afraid and by the time we reached the end of the driveway, I was sweating.

'Turn right along the road,' Mr Cool said from behind.

He didn't sound at all uncomfortable. Whenever I speeded up, he followed, without difficulty. He was on my shoulder all the way, breathing loudly but steadily through his mouth and I could hear the steady pounding of his feet. I noticed, as we began to climb before the descent to the village, that his footsteps were coming closer together. He wasn't moving faster though, he was taking shorter strides. I tried shortening my stride too and found it easier.

Suddenly he streamed past, moving dead easily it seemed, on tiptoe, so I tried that too and found it took the knife out of my calf muscles. I watched Mr Cool after that for more clues.

'This way,' he said, taking a sudden turn up a track signposted Greenwalls Farm.

He cut across me but I said nothing. It was easy

going on the farm-track. My mind began to drift and I pushed forward again. Mr Cool made no effort to stay ahead.

My mouth felt dry and yet full of spit at the same time. Sweat stung my eyes. I was running in the Olympics, running from the front in a mesh vest with the Union Jack in one corner. 'It's a brave run. He's led all the way,' I could hear Brendan Foster's voice. 'There's only half a lap to go. Can he —?' And there I was interrupted by the sound of a vehicle coming behind us.

Mr Cool must have heard it too because he jumped on to the grassy verge with a swear word that would have surprised Mum and Dad and everyone else.

It was, I noticed through the dust cloud as it passed us, a jeep, a white jeep, just like the jeep I'd seen last night. It reminded me that I was going to warn the farmer about the rustlers. I stopped and bent over, coughing and spluttering and wondered if I could make an excuse to stop at the farm.

''S rotten when that happens. Spoils your rhythm, doesn't it?'

'Yeah,' I said, coughing and spluttering some more to prove the point.

Mr Cool gurgled and spat neatly and stood with his hands on his hips waiting for me to recover. I noticed, thank goodness, that sweat was now pouring off him too, running down the sides of his eyes and bursting out of his nose. His chest was glowing.

That made me feel better, so I started off again and listened for his footsteps and tried to match them, which was stupid because his legs were twice as long as mine. I felt better for the rest but now my legs were tired. To stop thinking about them, I concentrated on the registration number of the jeep I'd seen last night. E something 3 or 8, something, something, S. That was it. An anonymous note, I decided, I could deliver it tonight.

We continued on the dried muddy track and reached the farm-house soon after. The farmer was just climbing out of his jeep. A sly-looking collie slunk to the ground and watched us run by, glancing at his master for instructions which didn't come.

The farmer was a ruddy-cheeked man with a cap and a friendly grin. And a white jeep, E43 NBS. So while Jack was calling out, 'Hello, Mr Cunnane!' I was thinking what a dumbo I'd have looked if I'd said anything. 'Rustling my own sheep!' I could imagine him chortling.

'Hello there,' he called. 'A bit warm, isn't it? Stop for a drink?'

But then, I thought, maybe he would like his torch back. I'd hidden it in my towel and taken it home in case my own batteries ran out. I hadn't figured anyone would bother about the torch but now I knew whose it was, somehow it was different – like stealing.

Mr Cool had pulled up. 'Want a drink?' he enquired.

I was about to say, 'Yes,' when, through a gap in the trees, I glimpsed the tower again, black and jagged against the blue sky and I felt all cold and said, 'No. No. I'm fine, thanks.'

There were all sorts of reasons for farmers like him to be out at night on their farms, but what on earth could he have been doing up in the tower?

'No, thanks,' Mr Cool called and we set off again.

'We turn off here,' he pointed. 'As long as we keep to the edge of the field, Mr Cunnane doesn't mind.'

We climbed a fence and Mr Cool led the way while I watched the cows and the cows watched us. What *had* Mr Cunnane been doing up that tower, I kept wondering.

At the end of the field, we climbed another fence and pushed through some bushes and trees until we reached the driveway.

Mr Cool moved nimbly and easily round the obstacles but I was stumbling now with tiredness and I couldn't concentrate for thinking about last night. At last, I lifted my head and saw the cottage, no more than two hundred metres away.

'I like to sprint this bit,' Mr Cool breathed.

And sure enough, he lowered his head and set off like a train. I tried to make my legs go faster. I tried to find the breath and the strength but there was nothing left. The swine!

I caught him where he'd flopped on the back lawn. The adults were sitting round one of the plastic tables having drinks. I was trembling but I wasn't sure why. My knees went and I fell beside Mr Cool, gasping.

'Good session,' he remarked casually, as much to the audience as to me.

I just lay face down in the grass and heard Josie's voice from the other side of the hedge, 'Time?'

'Thirty minutes,' Mr Cool said. 'About. You sure he doesn't run?'

'Yes,' said Dad quietly, but still didn't explain.

'He should,' said Mr Cool. 'He's a natural.'

He got up and went into the house to shower.

'Praise indeed,' Dad said. 'Maybe we'll find you a club when we get home, eh?'

I shrugged.

Only if I can be good enough to beat that swine, I thought.

Again, I went to bed before Mr Cool. There was a tap on the door. Fay came in wearing her summer nightdress. Her cheeks and nose were reddened by the sun, making her look tired and close to tears.

'Richard.'

'What?'

'About last night.'

She sat on Mr Cool's bed, twisting her fingers, her plump pink toes kneading the rug. I knew what she was going to say.

'Course I won't tell,' I said. 'None of my business.'

'Yeah, well.'

She sighed.

'I do try, Richard. During the day, when there are other people to remind me, it's easy. But at night I forget. I'm not really awake. I hardly know what I'm doing. You should've come in and stopped me.'

She looked so miserable and helpless.

'I didn't mean to be nasty about it,' I said. 'It was the fishing. I didn't want to do it. You were making me do it.'

Fay blushed.

'Josie's always had a brother,' she said, as though that explained everything.

She got up and stood in front of me while I stared at her feet on the fluffy rug and tried to work out what she meant. I felt I ought to feel sorry for her but I couldn't think why. She'd not had any brothers or sisters for so long. I'd always had someone, and usually too many. One of the foster homes had had six of us all in bunks like a dormitory.

'Well, goodnight then.'

It was a second before I realized she was going. I looked up quickly in time to meet her chin coming down to kiss me.

'Oof.'

'Sorry.'

She giggled and I giggled. She hugged me then but didn't kiss me.

'G'night.'

'G'night.'

I lay down again. She was really an OK sister, I thought, suddenly remembering my real sister, Ruth, with her white blond wispy curls, digging in the sandpit, shrieking when I'd driven my tricycle through her castles. I very nearly cried myself.

That was three times today I'd nearly cried. My mask was slipping. No, I vowed. No one will ever see me cry. No one can hurt me. I don't care. It doesn't matter, nothing matters. It doesn't matter, nothing matters.

I took a deep breath and began to plan what I'd do tonight, absent-mindedly picking up a screw of paper that had sailed out from under Mr Cool's bed when Fay shut the door. I lay on my back twisting and untwisting it, fiercely.

I'd awarded Mr Cool a point for his sprint finish, taken it off for poor sportsmanship, then had to award him another for praising me in front of everyone. The score now was 6–8 to him.

5

At five past three, I let myself into the kitchen and tiptoed to the back door.

I leant over the sink and pulled the pot towards me to look inside and the key slipped from beneath it into the sink. The sound was enormous. I switched off the light and waited, the key clenched in my fist. But no noise came from the rest of the house.

I took a deep breath, opened the door, slowly and gently and locked it behind me, slowly and gently. Then I let out the breath and began to tiptoe across the grass.

Suddenly, light flooded out of the kitchen window and across the lawn. Instinctively, I threw myself to the ground under the window, pinning myself against the rough, scratchy wall. Of course, Fay, in the kitchen, would not be able to see me, even if she did look elsewhere than the fridge and the biscuit tin, but I still pressed myself against that wall as though there were a hundred foot drop beside me.

Fay, I thought, banging the back of my head against the wall, Fay, Fay, stoppit. I can't come back in and stop you because you'd wonder what I'm doing out here in my clothes. Even if you are half asleep and don't notice now, you'll remember in the morning. Stop, stop, I know you know you don't want to eat. You're not hungry —

The light flicked off. That wasn't long. She must have got my message.

Rather pleased and, I suppose, a bit surprised, I pushed the key deliberately to the bottom of my pocket and patted it against my thigh. My eyes still not adjusted for carrot vision, I stood up and walked across the lawn. I found myself at the gate, so I opened it.

There was a cold breeze coming off the sea. I'd have liked to jog a bit to keep warm but I was afraid of slipping on the loose stones.

I stopped and humphed the way Fay and Josie did. I hadn't meant to come this way at all.

But I'd been to the castle and I wasn't interested in the cows and hay. I suddenly remembered when I'd first said that, 'Little Miss Muffet, Sat on her Tuffet, Eating her cows and hay,' and remembered how my old mum used to laugh, the kind of laugh that made everyone laugh, soft and round and jolly as she'd hugged me and repeated the joke to Dad.

Silly rhyme, stupid rhyme. It doesn't matter. Nothing matters.

Anyway, I wasn't interested in cows and actually, if I'd been honest, I'd have admitted to being slightly afraid of them. I don't understand them and they're big. But no one was there to force me to be honest so I just decided I wasn't interested.

I'd done the castle. The beach path was too danger-ous, so it had to be the village.

But somehow, here I was, feeling my way with my toes down the flipping beach path. I blamed Fay, distracting me with her midnight gobbling.

I worked out that when I got to the bottom of the steps, I'd go over the rocks towards the estuary and round to the village road.

In the days when I'd had to fend for myself, after my old mum had started getting drunk, or got ill or gone mad or whatever you called it, but before anyone had noticed enough to get me taken into care, I had learnt not to be impulsive, but to watch and listen and learn. I was careful. I had to be.

So when I reached the bottom of the path I paused. Ahead of me was a black shininess, like oil, as far as I could see. I dared flash on the torch and its beam slid across the sea for miles. The tide was right up, so high that the sand was completely covered. The lower steps were being licked by wavelets coming and falling back as though they couldn't make up their minds or didn't really care. 'It doesn't matter, nothing matters,' they seemed to be saying.

I hadn't noticed the cut-off to the fishing rock, it was so overgrown, and now it seemed there was nowhere to go.

This is stupid, I told myself. I can't see anything and I'm cold. But I'm free, for once, free of other people's expectations. I took a deep breath and watched the mist swirling over the gently rippling water. I shone the torch over the ebony black surface of the sea and thought it looked as if you could walk on it.

'I'm free,' I yelled, throwing my head back and shaking my fists at the vague brightness where the moon hid. I dumped myself down on the top step, my feet two steps lower and dared the waves to come higher.

I leant back and stared at the surface of the water. It was like blackcurrant jelly, an enormous pool of blackcurrant jelly. I closed my eyes and listened to it whispering to my feet, playing catch with my toes.

After a while, I looked at my watch. I was cold. It wouldn't be like a failure or a mistake if I went back now because I could get out any night I wanted. Last night I'd gone back because I was disturbed by Mr Cunnane dropping a torch on me. Well, not dropping a torch on me, OK I hadn't been hit. But the torch had definitely come from above, from up, up in the tower.

'Richard, you're so slow!' I shouted, springing to my feet. I turned to stare at the cliff and the castle rising out of the cliff but of course I couldn't see anything except a blackness against a grey sky. Up in the tower! There was a way up! Somewhere in the rubble, there must be a way up!

I felt dizzy with excitement. I began climbing the path, planning the games I could play if I could find the way up. Should I be a cunning attacker or a brave defender? By the time I reached the top, my legs were sore and my lungs ached and all I could do was flop over the garden gate, gasping for breath.

And Mr Cool *runs* that? I thought. I'd be a fool to try.

The horizon was looking pale. Yellow and blue it was. It didn't feel like night any more and I decided the adventure was definitely over for tonight. So I closed the gate carefully and tiptoed across the lawn. As I felt for the key I was quite happy, now that I had a goal for tomorrow night. But I couldn't find the key. Shoving my hand right in my pocket, I pulled the pocket inside out. All that was there was a hole. A small one, but big enough for a key. Rats!

I turned back to the gate. I searched every inch of that path with the torch, in the hope that a sparkle might catch my eye. Both down and up. I even fished around in the water on the bottom steps but the sea had retreated and I could hardly tell which ones had been covered.

By five o'clock, the sun was high enough to convince anyone it was daytime. I became more and more afraid of being discovered, so I gave up and climbed the path again, wondering how I was going to get back in. I was very tired and the idea of a warm, comfy mattress was very appealing.

The downstairs loo, as Fay called it, was the obvious window. It wasn't tall but it was wide. I would have to go through sideways. Trouble was, it was high up and directly over the lavatory pan.

43

Some families, I knew from experience, flushed the toilet whenever they went. But others didn't flush overnight in case the noise disturbed other people. I hoped, just in case I slipped, that Mr Cool came from the flushing variety.

I rested my chin on the window sill. The window was slightly open. It was the kind that pivoted, and pivoted on its long axis, making the gap even narrower. I just had to reach the safety catch at the top . . .

But I couldn't . . .

Yes I could.

Standing to one side and pulling myself up with one hand, I managed to reach in and flick it back. Gently, I pushed the window until it was fully open, then reached inside and moved the talc and shampoo and deodorant to one side. Pooh. I didn't like Mr Cool's deodorant.

I pulled myself up by the wooden sill but the window sticking out above my head meant I couldn't get the height to swing my leg over the sill. I dropped back to the grass and leant against the wall, my legs aching. I needed something to stand on.

Then I spotted one of the plastic chairs and dragged it over and was inside in no time. And joy of joys, the pan lid was down.

I rearranged the talc and shampoo and manky deodorant, set the safety catch and adjusted the window to the correct angle, took off my outdoor clothes and made my way back to the bedroom.

I could see clearly the shape of Mr Cool, his shoulders rising and falling evenly. I grinned. Another one to me. 7–8.

I placed my clothes neatly at the foot of the mattress and slid into my sleeping bag, all the while keeping one eye on Mr Cool.

But as I slid my foot inside the bag, it met something cold and slimy.

I had trained myself not to scream but to catch in my breath slowly and quietly. If you keep your face straight as well, no one can tell you've had a fright.

I unzipped the bag and looked inside. It was smeared with pink yoghurt and crumbled chocolate biscuits.

6

This wasn't Fay's style. Not for one second did I suspect her. Immediately I knew Mr Cool was the only possible culprit. Yet his shoulders still heaved steadily; there was not the slightest quiver to indicate a stifled giggle. Of course, I'd been out for two and a half hours so it was no wonder he'd gone back to sleep.

I wiped my foot clean on the sleeping bag and tiptoed through to the living-room. *The Galloway Gazette* and a small brass coal shovel sat beside the unused open fireplace. I picked them up and then collected the green sponge from the downstairs loo. Quietly, lying on the outside of the bag, so that I could duck down and pretend to be asleep if necessary, I scraped the worst of the mess on to the newspaper and sponged out the worst of the smell. It hadn't soaked in as much as I'd feared, or probably as much as Mr Cool had intended. The biscuits had absorbed much of the yoghurt. I'd never liked yoghurt. Three cheers for chocolate digestives.

I returned the sponge to the loo but couldn't think of a safe place to hide the newspaper, so in desperation I stuffed it under my mattress.

Having decided this was a plain nasty trick, not cool at all and so not worth any points, I went to sleep at six o'clock and had no difficulty ignoring the slight wet patch.

I was awakened by the sharp grinding of a sash window being hauled up. I turned slowly on my back and squinted at my cousin. He was standing at the open window, hands on his hips, breathing deeply.

You swine, I thought, before I'd even remembered why. My first impulse was to 'remain' asleep but then the door-key problem came back to me and I thought it would look suspicious if I weren't there. The best way of avoiding suspicion, I've learnt, is to discover the problem yourself.

I stretched and looked at my watch. It was eight fifteen. I pushed myself up on my elbows.

'Another beautiful morning, cuz.' Mr Cool grinned innocently and went out without waiting for a reply.

Immediately, I sprang up, snatched the newspaper and shovel and leapt out of the window, sprinting to the cover of the trees, remembering, as I hared across the dewy grass, that luckily no upstairs windows overlooked this side of the house.

I dug a hole with the shovel, buried the newspaper, wiped the shovel on some leaves and dashed back, reflecting how much easier this window was to negotiate than the downstairs loo. I sank on my mattress, my heart ticking like an unbalanced motorbike.

Suddenly my blood turned cold. The chair! I'd left the chair outside the downstairs loo. As soon as anyone went outside, which they were likely to do soon, because, although I hated to agree with Mr Cool, it looked like another fine morning, they would see it.

For now I had to return the coal shovel, so I pulled on my clothes and was tying my trainers by the time Mr Cool stuck his head and an arm round the door and threw his pyjama trousers on his bed with a cry of 'bathroom's free now' and a disgusted look at me for dressing without washing.

While Mr Cool was in the kitchen, I replaced the coal shovel. No one else seemed to be moving yet. I didn't want to go into the kitchen with no one there but Mr Cool and me. On the other hand, I did wonder how he was going to handle me. So I pushed open the door and looked out of the window which gave me a side view of him.

'Want some coffee?'

I shrugged. What've you put in it, you swine? I wondered.

'Shall I pour some out for you or not?'

'Um . . .'

'Well, it's here if you want it.'

'OK, thanks.'

'I don't want you to strain yourself but would you like some toast?'

'Yes, please.' You can't do much to toast while I'm watching.

'I'm having breakfast when I get back. Decided

to do today's training early, before it gets too hot. Want to come?'

'I, um, I thought I'd do the beach path run today.'

'Well, whatever. But remember to walk it first. I don't want you killing yourself and anyone saying I made you do it. Toast's ready.'

Mr Cool took his own, shoved it dry into his mouth and held it between his teeth as he lifted his coffee mug and went to the back door. I dived at the cooker, then the fridge in search of margarine, then at the cupboards in search of lemon curd. I started whistling to blot out the sound of Mr Cool's search for the key.

He took the toast out of his mouth and turned to face me, his eyes on the ceiling, his foot tapping on the floor.

'Oh, dear,' he announced, slowly and clearly and menacingly. 'I can't seem to find the key. Do you, Richard, have any idea where it might possibly be?'

I looked at the door, shrugged and turned back to my toast.

'Come on, Richard. I won't tell anyone. I just want the sodding key!'

His voice hardened and rose in a very uncool way. I felt it might be wise to keep an eye on him.

'I don't know where it is.'

He rolled his eyes.

'They warned me you were a compulsive liar. All right. Have it your own way. You *weren't* out wandering in the middle of the night.'

49

I hadn't said that. However, I now thought it safe to turn my back on him and start putting things away.

'Do I have to search your pockets?'

I turned round and pulled out the pockets of my jeans with a flourish.

Mr Cool shook his head.

'OK, OK. It doesn't matter. I'll go out the front door. You can replace it before anyone comes. But listen, cuz,' he lifted a warning finger, 'the castle's barely safe by day and certainly not at night. You getting killed would really spoil everyone's holiday.'

'But I didn't go to the castle.'

'Aw, don't waste my time,' he said with an air of overstrained patience. 'I'm off.' He tipped his coffee into the sink. 'Just get that key back and don't go to the castle again at night.'

For the first time, I regretted my mask. I felt genuinely surprised and it would have been useful to look it. 'Maybe you just didn't look properly,' I said to the closed door.

What was the point of telling the truth? I didn't know where the key was and I hadn't been to the castle last night. But Mr Cool didn't believe me on either count because he'd been told I was a compulsive liar.

The front door closed. I ran through the hall, opened the front door and saw Mr Cool jogging out of sight round the bend. I sprinted round the house and grabbed the chair, then walked casually across the lawn to place it with the set. Half-way across the lawn, a cheery voice hailed me from above.

'You're up early. It's a fine day.'

'Oh, I was just rescuing the chair,' I replied, turning to squint up at the window where Uncle Steve was doing his breathing exercises. 'It seems to have blown round our side of the house.'

'Right.'

Minutes later, Uncle Steve materialized in the kitchen, dressed only in a pair of baggy shorts.

'Some wind!'

'Huh?'

'To blow the chair away.'

I looked out of the window. The sun shone. There wasn't a cloud moving in the sky. The bushes weren't even twitching.

'Breakfast in bed for the ladies,' Uncle Steve announced. 'They're supposed to be on holiday. Like to help? By the way, why did you come in the front door?'

'I couldn't find the back-door key,' I said, wishing I'd got that in first.

'It's just here,' smiled Uncle Steve, then, 'Oh! Who locked up? I think it was your dad. He must've put it somewhere else. Bit of a rebel, your dad.'

I looked at Uncle Steve to see if he was joking. But everything Uncle Steve said sounded like a huge joke. I continued laying the tray with cereal. 'I'll take Dad's too,' I said, pouring orange juice into the glasses.

'That's the tea brewing.'

51

'I'll get it when I come back for the toast. They like their toast hot.'

Uncle Steve looked impressed.

I pushed the bedroom door open with my foot, thankful it wasn't closed. First Dad, then Mum surfaced and blinked in surprise, then struggled to arrange themselves sitting up in bed. Dad patted down the covers over his knees.

'Dad, do you know where the back-door key is?'

'Under the flowerpot.'

'It isn't.'

Dad yawned and rubbed his stubble.

'Must've slipped down the back or something.'

'Richard! How lovely!' Mum beamed. 'How sweet!'

'It was Uncle Steve's idea. He's taking breakfast to Auntie Chris.'

'Not Jack?'

'He's gone for a run before it gets too hot.'

Mum nodded as if something about that satisfied her, as if, perhaps, she was pleased that Mr Cool hadn't brought Auntie Chris breakfast in bed but I had brought hers.

One up to me, I thought. 8 all and counting. What a beautiful morning.

'Maybe he took the key.'

'Maybe he did — I mean no! He was looking for it before he left.'

'I expect it'll turn up.'

'Yeah. I'll fetch the tea and toast. Then I'm going to try Jack's path.'

'Be careful, Richard.'

'I'll walk it first.'

I closed the door and listened.

'*Jack's* path!' Mum muttered in disgust.

So! The impressive Jack McPherson doesn't impress everyone!

I put on my stopwatch and walked slowly and carefully down the path. One way and another, I knew it quite well by now. My thigh muscles ached and protested as I tottered down the slope, threatening to rip with each step.

I had some kind of an idea that I might just find the key – but I couldn't think where to say I'd found it. I also had to remember to go back with realistic times for the path run. Mr Cool had claimed six minutes for downhill and eleven for uphill, Josie eight twenty-two and fifteen five. Mine should be somewhere in the middle.

By now I had reached the bottom of the path, where the steps began. Last night there had been three steps clear. Now they were all clear and the sea had retreated almost out of sight.

I began jogging up the path but my calf muscles felt wooden. They wouldn't respond. I tried taking shorter steps on tiptoe but there was little relief so I shut out the pain with my mantra. Hands on knees, I growled at myself and teased myself. Just the next bend. Just the next bush, just to that big stone, just to the gate. The gate. I hung over it, gasping with relief.

Then I remembered I was supposed to run

down as well. No way. I limped part way then slid off to one side under a bush and waited for twenty minutes before making a show of the return trip. I stood up, gasping and let myself in the gate.

Mum was at the sink. I made a sign that looked like a key turning in a lock. She shrugged and spread her hands wide and seemed to splash someone because she looked away and laughed. I went to the front door, came in and showered then went to the dining-room and announced my times as seven forty and thirteen twenty-six.

'Took it easy,' I said, rubbing my thighs, 'the first time.'

'If you're stiff, a swim will help,' said Mr Cool not looking up from a plate of ham, eggs, tomatoes and mushrooms.

I was ravenous and shut my nostrils against the smell.

'Richard, you haven't been raiding the fridge have you? I mean, you didn't get hungry in the middle of the night?'

I looked at Auntie Chris, whose T-shirt today demanded that we save trees, and shook my head, hoping I looked as though I hadn't a clue what she was talking about.

'No? Only some yoghurts have gone. And another packet of chocolate biscuits. I had the right number for lunch. Now I'll have to nip out and buy more.'

I looked accusingly at Fay. She'd expect that. A high spot appeared on her cheeks and her eyes looked anguished. She shook her head and mouthed no. I shrugged.

'All right. You don't have to own up. But I just want to make the point that it's inconvenient. If anyone does want to nibble, would they please take something there's plenty of.'

'Yes ma'am,' said Uncle Steve with a salute, making even Auntie Chris laugh.

I longed to look at Mr Cool, to see what he was making of all this.

'Good run, Rich,' Mr Cool said, getting up from the table. 'But watch you don't get dehydrated.' He sauntered across the room. 'Check your urine. If it gets dark drink loads.' His hand was on the door handle.

'Thanks for the tip,' I said.

'Yoghurt won't help,' he added, sailing out of the room.

Mentally, I threw six cartons of yoghurt after him and enjoyed the sight of him dripping hazelnut and orange and strawberry and banana until the smell made my stomach heave.

I felt betrayed that no one in the family had spoken up for me and said I didn't like yoghurt.

7

The swim turned out to involve a walk to the village, where an open air tidal pool was carved out of the rocks on the far side of the harbour.

Auntie Chris managed to buy the extra yoghurt and we sat on the tiered seats to eat lunch. I did not eat any yoghurt but if anyone noticed I expect they thought it was because I'd had too many during the night.

We walked to the end of the pier, Fay avoiding me quite pointedly, to watch the start of the yacht race.

Uncle Steve checked his watch. 'They have about two hours before the tide turns.'

'When does the tide turn? How do you know?' asked Josie.

'Oh, we experts know these things,' he said with a wink.

'The rest of us look up the tide tables,' said Dad and everyone laughed. 'They're on display at the hut there.'

'Good turn out,' commented Mum.

I followed her gaze to the harbour where about fifty yachts were trying to bring themselves to a line level with the pier. There were shouts of warning, laughter and annoyance. It looked impossible. But colourful, with the yachts' bright sails.

Suddenly, without warning, a gun went off and the boats began to move more purposefully.

'Look at that poor soul,' Mum cried. 'He's still going backwards.'

'Here come the rafts now,' said Auntie Chris.

The rafts were arriving by trailer and by hand. Barrels and planks, tied together with rope and twine and painted with silly names like *West End Wanderer, Ducky Lucky* and *Beauty of Bath*, this being an old bath surrounded by plastic barrels.

'Look. There's Mr Cunnane,' Josie shouted, pointing at the white jeep which was backing its trailer down to the slipway. The ruddy-faced farmer leant out of the cab, a cigarette hanging out of his mouth, checking his progress carefully.

He caught sight of us.

'Hi there. I'm needing some crew. Come and help us?'

Mum and Dad and Auntie Chris and Uncle Steve laughed as though they'd been expecting it.

'Go on, Richard. Go on,' cried Josie and Fay, pushing me towards the slipway.

I edged to the side. Not with him.

'Come on, Richard,' Mr Cunnane called. 'You can make a fool of yourself too.'

'Aw, go on Richard,' cried Josie.

I wondered where Mr Cool was. Surely Jack the hero would step into the breach. Actually, it looked a bit of a laugh. Clearly, not many of the rafts would survive and that was part of the fun. But not with him. I couldn't face Mr Cunnane.

'Oh, is that the rafts?' said Mr Cool, just coming out of the gents. 'Great.'

And that decided me.

'I'm still too stiff,' I protested. 'It's not my scene.'

I shook myself free of the girls and walked away as though nothing much was happening there. I wandered down to the hut and examined the tide tables, thinking how nice it would be if they were wrong and Mr Cunnane's raft was swept out to sea with Mr Cool on it.

There was an asterisk against Sunday's table. That meant there was a full moon, which apparently gave the highest tide of the month. A ten-foot tide. The difference between high and low tide, I supposed.

I began to think about tonight's trip to the tower. And then remembered Mr Cool's warning. What had made him think I'd been to the castle?

Shouts and cheers greeted me as I wandered back to join the others. The race was under way.

'Jack's on Mr Cunnane's raft,' Josie announced proudly.

Fay looked at me, pulled an expression of disgust, then turned to watch the race.

I knew I had failed her.

I went to the kiosk to buy some gum and by the time I came back, all the rafts had sunk except *Ducky Lucky*.

*

That night, the heavens opened.

I watched the rain dashing against the windows and streaming down. It was a relief, in a way, not to be able to go out tonight. I was exhausted and had barely stayed awake over dinner. All I was looking forward to was a good night's sleep but there remained the problem of the sleeping bag, so I carried my cocoa through to the bedroom and spilt it on my sleeping bag and pyjamas and went back to the living-room and asked if there was a spare sleeping bag. I knew there was. I'd seen it in the cupboard under the stairs.

The smelly sleeping bag was put to soak over-night in the bath and I got a clean one.

Mr Cool gave me a knowing smile.

Propped up and comfortable now, in clean pyjamas and a clean sleeping bag and with a Beano annual, I looked sideways at my cousin, lying there so cool and confident.

'Jack?'

'Uhuh.' He didn't look up.

'Why did you say I'd been to the castle last night?'

'I saw your map.'

Bor-ing, his tone implied. He turned on his back, bent his knees and held the book over his head.

There was no point denying I had a map. The swine must have seen something.

'What did you do with it?'

'I read it and put it back on your bed.'

59

Rats! My bed was now soaking in the upstairs bathroom.

'But it's not here now.'

'So look. It's probably on the floor – yeah – look. There.'

I followed the vague direction of Mr Cool's nod. All I could see was the screw of paper I'd found under his bed. Keeping my eyes sideways on him, I got out of bed and picked it up. I knew he was watching me. I untwisted the screw.

There was a square building with circles in each corner and a vertical line on the left, curving towards a semi-circle in front of the castle and continuing to run parallel to itself. There was a square at the end of one line that must be the lodge cottage and another a little way up that must be our cottage. On the other road, there was a big square that represented the farm.

'Your map, not mine,' I said, preparing to take a point. 'It was under your bed.'

'Hardly mine,' Mr Cool said with a sigh. 'There's too much wrong with it. It's not to scale. The cross is in the wrong tower. I'd have shown the difference between the main road and the driveway and I'd also have shown the path to the beach. No. Definitely more your style.'

I looked at it again. There was a cross in the incomplete tower on the sea wall. The *wrong* tower, Mr Cool had called it. So he knew you could get up the other one.

'What's Sheet 84GR 869528?' I asked.

'Very funny.'

'No, come on. What's it mean?'

'You should know.'

'I didn't draw this. I found it under your bed. Probably the last people left it.'

'Oh, here we go again! Sheet 84 is the ordnance survey sheet number for this area and GR is the grid reference number for a particular place, in this instance Greenwalls Castle. At least you got that much right even if your drawing's pathetic.'

'But I didn't . . .'

'Oh, give me strength.'

Mr Cool threw down his book and stamped out of the room. He wasn't walking out on me like that. I followed.

'Is there a map here?' I asked in the kitchen.

'In the study.'

I tiptoed past the living-room where I could hear the reassuring hum of voices. In the study was a small sofa, a desk, a table in the bay window and two bookshelves. The room had a quiet atmosphere, as though it was hardly ever used. A painting above the mantelpiece caught my eye. It showed a wild and furious sea, yellow green against a purple grey sky, spitting foam over black rocks. Another painting on the opposite wall showed the sea in the foreground, a rocky promontory and a castle towering above it. It must have been painted from the other side of the bay.

'Grief! Now he's pretending he doesn't know where the maps are!' exclaimed Mr Cool.

He went straight to the bookcase on the right of the window, lowered himself, straight-backed, without spilling his coffee and fingered out the map. He threw it across the sofa back and it slid off.

I sent him a dirty look as I picked it up and opened it out, again and again, until it was huge and unmanageable, like what Dad called a 'proper' newspaper. I tried to rest it on the table but it kept slipping off, so I pushed the northern part out of the way and studied the coastline along the bottom, aware of Mr Cool watching me.

Dumfries. That was the nearest town. I found that. Then south to the village and yes, I traced the yellow village road and the white tracks that were the driveways to the farm and to the cottage. They actually formed a loop with the castle at the join.

'What puzzles me, cuz, is why you do it? Why you lie? Why we're going through this charade? I mean, so what if you look up the castle on the map? I've always been fascinated by it myself. But I never went there in the dark. I always went with everyone else when we went for a walk, or with Josie and Fay to play and explore.

'They were always damsels in distress, you see, imprisoned by their cruel uncle in the tower. (We were never sure whether the cruel uncle was your dad or mine.) Anyway, I of course, had to rescue them and fall in love with them. A bit much having to fall in love with 'em both but what the hell? It was a game. I liked the castle. I knew every inch of it. Sometimes I left them there for ages before I rescued them . . .'

He seemed embarrassed.

'So,' he continued after a swig of coffee, 'why pretend you're not an ordinary kid, like me and anyone else, who wants to explore the castle. We can go there any day you want.'

'It's not my map. Get it? I didn't draw it,' I shouted, suddenly trembling with an anger that was taking away my breath. I couldn't control it. I stood and stared out of the window, my fists clenched at my sides, my shoulders tight up to my ears. It doesn't matter, nothing matters. It doesn't matter, nothing matters.

'Pardon?' said Mr Cool. 'Your lips are moving. Never mind. It doesn't matter.' He sighed. 'They thought because I'm a boy, I might be able to get close to you.'

I felt dizzy now. I let myself breathe but had to grip the table to stop myself swaying. I tried to read Mr Cool's tone. It might have been sarcastic. It might have been disappointed. Probably it was both. Probably he wanted company as much as I did.

But actually, that seemed unlikely. Mr Cool had been the hero, the knight in shining armour, for as long as they'd all been coming here, which was for ever as far as I could tell. And now there was another, a rival. Me.

I clenched my teeth even harder to stop myself shaking.

63

'Cold? Better get back to bed. I'll put away the map.'

He took a couple of steps towards me but I spun round whipping an imaginary gun up from my hip. Mr Cool's hands slowly lifted in surrender, the cup held steady, the eyes narrowing. The map slid to the floor. Neither of us moved. Something hammered in my brain, something that wanted out. I was losing control. I was losing control.

'Richard, we all know you've had a hard time. I don't know the details but whatever happened is over now. There's no need to behave like this. All suspicious. As though everyone were out to get you.'

He waved the hand with the mug in it but kept both hands over his head.

'You're making it harder, worse, for everyone.'

I wasn't listening. This stupid older boy was actually standing there with his hands up because he was scared of my pretend gun. There was something incredibly funny about that. Like people being fooled by a finger in the back. I'd seen that on television.

But Mr Cool wasn't fooled. And he wasn't scared. He was humouring me. He thought we were playing a game.

'Look, how're you ever going to make friends if you lie to people?' he was saying.

You should see yourself, I thought, playing games with someone who isn't playing games. You think I'm playing games?

64

'You lie to *yourself*. That's the trouble.'

I laughed, because Mr Cool was saying what everyone said, the social workers, the psychologists, the teachers. It was really funny coming from him too.

'Not funny,' Mr Cool said. 'True. First you lie to yourself so that lies are truth and that means you aren't lying to other people. But lying to yourself . . . That is so sad. How can anyone get close to you?'

He shook his head, yes sadly, put his cup on the table and bent to pick up the map.

I jerked the pretend gun but he wasn't looking. He was finding the creases to fold the map. Ignoring me. Ignoring me! So I brought the gun crashing down on the back of his skull and ran out of the room.

If the truth is so bad, why not pretend, why not? Why suffer? That's what my old mum used to say. 'Just a little drink, Richard, helps me to bear it. Just a little one. Just one.'

I couldn't drink. I couldn't hide that way. Besides, I knew that kind of hiding was stupid. In the first place, it didn't last because you woke up. In the second place, you woke up with a splitting headache. In the third place it needed money. And in the fourth place, people despised you.

'No one loves a drunk,' Mum had admitted after that boyfriend left.

'Dad loved you,' I'd said.

Mum hadn't always been a drinker.

8

I woke, next morning, facing into the room. I
listened but couldn't make out whether Mr Cool
was still asleep so I opened one eye. My cousin
was lying on his back staring at the ceiling. His
hands cushioned his head. He looked annoyed
and sad and determined and fed up all at once.
Then he took a deep breath and swung his legs
over the bed. As he sat up, he caught sight of me
and I knew I hadn't time to close my eyes. Besides,
it might unnerve the swine if he thought I'd been
watching him.

'Sunshine, cuz. Storm's over.'

I wondered if he meant the weather.

'C'm'on. I'll take you to the castle today. We
can have a rotten princess each if they want to
come.'

He ground up the window and took a deep
breath of sea air then turned and looked down at
me. He pulled his lips together tightly and his eyes
dulled. Then he took another deep breath and
said, 'Please?'

Wow! What an effort!

I pushed back the covers and nodded.

Mr Cool went to wash and I picked up the map

scrap again. It seemed there was a piece torn off. I listened to make sure Mr Cool was still busy, then wriggled under his bed and felt in the dust.

I found one red sock, a girly magazine and then my fingers closed on something hopeful but it turned out to be a sweet wrapper. Moving up, I found another and then something else. I hid the magazine under my mattress for later and examined the paper.

The tear matched. 0315 13891. It was just a phone number!

There was something strange about drawing a map and then pretending someone else had done it. Maybe the phone number was his secret girl-friend's. I grinned. There was one way to find out.

'Coming then?' asked Mr Cool after breakfast. 'If we go now, we can go to the beach this after-noon. I want to work on my tan.'

'Go where?'

'To the castle of course.'

'Oh, are you going to the castle?' said Mum wistfully. 'The children used to play there all the time when they were younger. Remember, Chris?'

'Suppose I said I didn't want to go?' I hissed as we went out of the hall.

'I wouldn't believe you. Got any other ideas?'

Put on the spot like that, of course I hadn't. And even if I had, they wouldn't have included him.

'I didn't go for a run this morning. Mind if we do it on the way? It's about four to the castle by the road and two back.'

What sort of challenge was this?

'We'll just take it easy,' he said.

We took the same route as before, except instead of cutting across the fields, we stayed on the farm track until it curved hard right and suddenly there were the ruins of the castle.

'You took that slower,' Mr Cool commented as he stopped, hardly out of breath.

'Could've gone quicker.'

'I know. You can't fool me about these things.'

I was just wondering if that was worth half a point when he nodded at the far side of the castle, its shadows black and gruesome.

'That's the tower you can climb, not the one you marked.'

I opened my mouth and shut it again.

'Want to go up?'

I nodded.

First we had to scramble over the rubble of the front walls. It was odd the way one tower was so perfect and the rest so devastated. You couldn't imagine how it had happened.

'How did it happen?' I asked.

'What?'

'The fire – or whatever it was?'

'Dunno.'

So you don't know everything, Mr Smart Alec.

'It was long before we started coming.'

There was a clearer part in the middle. I stopped there because I wanted to look round. The tower looked so special, so impressive, so memorable that I wanted to keep it till last.

'You go on,' I said. 'I'll catch you up.'

'Just say if you need a pee,' Mr Cool said disgustedly. But he went on even so.

I looked round for something slightly more inspiring to do. I clambered about some more, identifying rooms and imagining them floored and furnished, with people wearing grand clothes, ladies in puffed-out dresses and men in tights and buckled shoes and wigs. It wasn't that big a castle but it didn't matter. A castle was a castle.

In one end wall, a gaping hole formed a fireplace and lath and plaster still clung to the stone. It had a pale green tinge. Overlooking the sea, enough wall remained to hold a window with a charred wooden frame. I went across to it and pushed my head through the window. The view made me dizzy. How could they have built straight up from the rocks like this? I forced myself to look. It was like forcing myself to jump.

Mr Cool shouted from the tower.

'It's no worse up here. Don't be scared!'

'I'm not.' I'm just petrified.

'There are only sixty-seven steps.'

'Good.'

The tide was still out. You could see England across the Solway Firth. The hills of the Lake District cut into the blue sky. I ducked my head back in, curious to know why the cross had been at the other tower, and scrambled across the inside of the castle to get to it. I found a wooden door, which I pushed open easily. A gust of cold air washed my face.

'You can't get up that one,' came the shout again.

Mr Cool's head was in a narrow slit at the top of the big tower. Shut up, I thought. Can't I look? You've had years to look. Leave me alone.

'I'm just looking.'

I looked. There were a few steps but you could tell they didn't go anywhere. Now you know, I told myself. It was just a mistake. I went back to the complete tower. The windows were tiny and the walls thick.

No, you swine. I'm not coming to your whistle, I decided, suddenly veering to the outside. I walked round the path to the edge of the castle and to the barrier where I'd been that night. I saw again the big wooden plank across the end of the path with DANGER painted on it and a skull and crossbones. What *had* Mr Cunnane been up to? I couldn't help being curious, suspicious, even. I looked down and tried to work out exactly where the torch had dropped. The base of the cliffs seemed to sink into the sand. I looked up and tried to identify the window where Mr Cunnane must have been standing and when I thought I had it, I turned back.

I pushed open the door of the big tower and instantly was hit by a cold staleness. The stairs corkscrewed upwards. My eyes took some time to get used to the gloom, so I trailed my hand along the wall until my fingers were rubbed sore. At the top was a small, square room.

70

'There ought to be a flag,' said Jack. 'Don't you think?'

He looked sad, somehow, as if he had lost something.

'S'pose so.'

'Some view.'

I tried one window, which looked down on the inside of the castle and guessed we were about four storeys high.

'How old is this place?'

'Sorry. I'm not into history.'

I noticed the door I had left open at the base of the other tower was now swinging. I turned to a different window, overlooking the sea. The wind punched me in the face as I leant out but I didn't draw back.

The extra height was fantastic, the view brill! You could see along the coast for miles. Round at the harbour, the yachting types were getting ready for the tide turning. I hitched myself on to the window sill and wriggled forward. Mr Cool grabbed my waistband, even though the window was too narrow for me to have fallen through.

'Hey, take it easy!'

I peered over the edge. Straight down was the barrier, where I'd been standing when Mr Cunnane had dropped the torch.

'I hope you don't carry on like this when you come here at night,' Mr Cool said.

He adjusted his grip, his fingers warm and soft in the small of my back, contrasting with the stone against my stomach that was hard, cold and so solid. I squirmed back and slid to my feet.

'I've never been up here before,' I said.

Mr Cool looked away in disgust.

'Want to stay?'

I shook my head.

'I've seen what I wanted to see.'

We arrived back at the cottage in time to see the white jeep leaving.

'Mr Cunnane?' Mr Cool asked. 'Was he pleased with the raft then?'

'Hardly,' laughed Uncle Steve.

'But I'm sure we got at least a hundred metres farther than last year.'

Uncle Steve grinned.

'Actually it was Mrs Cunnane. She brought a couple of chaps who were here last week for the fishing and reckoned they'd lost something.'

'Fishermen!'

'Bright lad. You worked that out all by yourself!'

Mr Cool made a face at his father.

'It was in your room,' Uncle Steve said. 'They found it, whatever it was.'

'You mean you let them in there alone? My fishing rod!'

He rushed into the house and along to our room. I was about to follow but Dad stopped me. Uncle Steve suddenly remembered he'd promised to tidy the living-room. What? I thought. Then Dad waved the girly magazine at me.

'They found this under your mattress, Richard.'

I stared at the smiling girls on the front cover.

'I suppose it's only natural,' Dad said, walking away from me, 'but I'm disappointed, Richard. I don't think you're quite old enough for this. I'm keeping it.'

He wouldn't have believed me if I'd told him I'd found it under Mr Cool's bed so I muttered, 'Sorry,' and he let me go.

By the time I reached the bedroom, Mr Cool was calmly replacing his precious rod in the wardrobe.

''S OK,' he said, as if I cared.

I flopped on my mattress then sat up again.

'Look!'

I pointed at his bed.

He frowned. 'What? I don't see.'

'They took the map and phone number.'

'What phone number? Richard, you're at it again. It's no use hiding in your fantasy world. I'm not listening. Look, just cool it Richard. It's no big deal. Bags first shower.'

I watched him go. I'm not lying, I told the door. OK, so it wasn't your map. If you'd given me a chance, I'd have told you about the missing piece.

But that was the trouble. No one ever gave me a chance. Just because I like to think before I open my mouth. Usually.

But the door wasn't listening either so I imagined my fingers round Jack's neck, squeezing hard and his lightly tanned, spotty face turning darker and darker and redder – or bluer, I couldn't decide which, until his spots burst.

The rest of the day went easily enough and in the evening the adults got out the cards.

'Last year at school then?' Dad said to Mr Cool.

They were playing bridge and Dad was dummy. Mum said it made her nervous when he watched her playing, so he had to find someone to chat with.

'Aw, give us a chance,' protested Mr Cool who was following the game. 'I'm on holiday, remember?'

'Well since the only time I ever see you is when we're on holiday, there isn't much alternative.'

'I'm thinking of joining the army, actually,' Mr Cool announced.

I stopped chewing my slice of cake and the plate dropped out of my fingers.

'They pay you through university you see . . .' he went on, ignoring my clumsiness.

But Dad knew it wasn't clumsiness. So did Mum. The game stopped.

'Richard's father was in the army,' explained Mum.

'Oh, really,' Mr Cool said with innocent interest. 'Where?'

'In the garden,' I replied.

'Belfast,' said Mum.

Usually – always – people had been told all this

beforehand, by the social workers, psychologists and teachers to whom I was 'a case' or by Mum or Dad, wanting to avoid what they called 'upsetting indiscretions' – such as this.

'What did he do?' Mr Cool went on, for once addressing me as if I were capable of answering.

'Nothing. He was gardening.'

'Gardening?'

'I mean he was in the infantry.'

'What Richard means, Jack,' Mum said softly, 'is that his father was gardening – in the garden – when he was killed. A terrorist shot him.'

'Aw no!' the prat gasped. 'I – I'm sorry. I didn't know. Gosh how awful!'

I felt sorry for him because he looked pretty shocked but I looked straight back without expression. The words of my mantra kept me from going mad.

'Did you . . . Were you there?' Josie asked.

I thought for a moment because I'd already told her – at least agreed with her – that my parents had been killed in a car crash. I said, in a loud, clear voice, 'We were all there. My mother was shot in the leg and the ricochet that killed my little sister grazed my arm.'

I rolled up my sweatshirt for anyone to see but no one looked.

Auntie Chris's hands flew to her cheeks and she gave a little sob. Mum's eyes overflowed with tears and she fumbled in her brown leather handbag for a tissue. Uncle Steve cleared his throat and shook his head. Fay and Josie exchanged looks of horror. Mr Cool stared at the floor.

'Well done, Richard,' Dad said, gruffly. 'That's the first time I've heard you talk about it. You can, you know, if you want to. You shouldn't lock up your feelings about it.'

'It's the first time I've had to.'

Mum gave a gentle cough. 'Would you rather it was like that? That you told people yourself?'

I considered this. I didn't like being a case, being talked about behind my back. But I didn't like the weeping women around me now, acting as if I was a character in a TV soap. They got a kick out of it. I wished they would keep their tears to themselves.

'Doesn't matter,' I shrugged. Nothing matters, I added, to myself.

I looked at my watch, stood up and said good-night. Then I went straight to my room without listening at the door.

9

I'd planned to read. If I was to have a chance at running, I'd have to catch up with this blinking school work. And that meant reading. But the words blurred before my eyes. My hands trembled. I dropped the book and let my head fall back on the pillow.

There was a knock at the door. I sat upright and grabbed at the book. Fay came in.

'Goodnight, Richard,' she said. 'I'm proud of you for telling the truth.'

'I don't blame you for lying,' said Josie over her shoulder.

'There's no point, though, is there,' I said.

Fay kissed me and they left.

There was no point, when there were so many misunderstandings with the truth, I thought angrily, remembering the map, the phone number, the girly magazine.

After another meaningless paragraph, I decided it was a bad time to start, so I put the book on the floor and snuggled into the sleeping bag.

But I couldn't sleep.

The men with the map and phone number puzzled me. Why did they need those pieces of paper? Directory Enquiries don't charge if you call from a phone box. And the grid reference number of the castle was easy to work out – once you knew how. It was very odd, far more interesting than the fact that Mr Cunnane, even if he did give me the creeps, liked going for walks in the middle of the night, just like me.

There was one way I might find out. And that was to phone the number. I hadn't had a chance today. OK, so it wasn't Mr Cool's secret girlfriend, which would have been much more fun, but it was odd and worth investigating, when you found a phone number for a ruined castle. Tomorrow I would phone the number and find out who was so interested in the 'wrong' tower and, if I were clever with my questions, why.

On Saturday, we climbed into cars and had a day out at a forest park where we picnicked, walked and admired trees. I didn't try to use my mantra, allowing myself to be irritable and grumpy. I suspected that, somehow, I had outgrown its power.

Over and over again, I heard my voice repeating, 'We were all there. My mother was shot in the leg and the ricochet that killed my little sister grazed my arm.'

And when I looked into my memory, I could see it all so clearly; the flash from the gun, Dad suddenly crumpling and falling, his head burst all over the grass; Ruth, her mouth and eyes open wide with surprise, the red fountain coming out of

78

her dress; Mum's face twisted in horror as she looked up from her magazine, stood up, then clutched her leg and fell, her mouth forming angry words. The video rewound and repeated itself all day, with no sound.

People left me alone.

The only voice that got through to me was the policeman's voice – 'How many shots, Richard? How many shots did you hear? Did he say anything? Anything at all?' I'd cried because I didn't know. 'Please try and help us. Anything you can remember, any small thing, might just be what we need to finish the jigsaw.' I remembered the blackbirds going up and Ruth's daisy chain breaking; I remembered the man's back as he ran away down the street but nothing that was of use. And so it was my fault that they never caught him.

That evening, we walked to the local hotel. It had tables and chairs in the garden and a view of the harbour and the yachts that were tying up for the night. Fay and Josie took themselves off to the playground but soon tired of that and found a quiet corner. Mr Cool sat with the adults, thinking he was dead cool with his shades, black T-shirt, black jeans and shandy.

I found the public telephone in the foyer and waited till it was free. But the connection wouldn't work. Frustrated, I returned to the table, to see that two men had joined us. They had Irish accents and were talking fishing with Mr Cool. I didn't like the accents, so I skirted the tables and went to sit on the wall until midges drove everyone indoors. I went back to the family as the Irishmen left. The taller man had black hair and a curly beard and looked like a pirate. His eyes were cold and grey, in spite of the smiling mouth, eyes that lied. It takes one to know one.

'Those were the gentlemen who were in Greenwalls Cottage last week,' Mum explained.

And who came back for a dodgy map and a dodgy phone number, I thought, my fists clenching in frustration at the missed chance.

I just wanted to sleep when I went to bed. It was a kind of hiding. But Fay was calling me and pulling me.

I woke up pushing her away, my eyes protesting at the light she had switched on.

'Those two Irishmen are back. They're trying to start their car. They're pushing it. They need a hand. Come on!'

Mr Cool was receiving the same treatment from Josie, but had managed to grab her wrists.

'They were going fishing,' he said, his speech slurred from sleep.

'Yes, well they're not going anywhere just now. They're pushing their car to bump start it. They're pushing it up to the castle!' Josie exclaimed.

'I'm not helping them!' I said. 'Leave me alone.'

'Why not?' Fay whispered indignantly.

'They're Irish!'

'You can't hate everyone who's Irish.'

I looked at my watch.

'It's two o'clock.'

'Yeah. Why don't you get Dad and Uncle Bill?' Mr Cool suggested. 'Why us?'

He was sitting up now.

'I thought you'd prefer the adventure,' Josie answered pertly.

'Cheek!'

He swung his legs out of bed and pulled on his jeans over his pyjamas. He found his T-shirt and pulled a jumper out of the drawer.

'They must be trying to catch the tide. Don't bother, Richard. We'll probably manage. But I wonder where they're going? Maybe they'd let me go too. I've never been fishing at night.'

'Jack! Don't you dare! That's not fair! You should . . .'

'Yes, I know. I should OK it with the folks first. Calm down. Of course I wouldn't.'

Josie humphed with her arms folded and watched her brother tying his trainers. Fay sat, quiet with disappointment, on the end of my mattress.

Mr Cool pulled up the window, slowly, so that it made a low sliding noise instead of its usual growling dash. He climbed through and Josie started to follow.

A hand came back through the window and a finger tapped her shoulder.

'No!' said Mr Cool. 'Girls shouldn't be wandering about at night, especially in nighties. Go back to bed.'

Josie pulled another humph at him. There was a glint of rebellion in her narrowed eyes. I wouldn't have trusted her.

'Come on, Fay. I hope he freezes out there.'

They trooped out of the room, forgetting me. I had to get up and switch off the light.

Next time, I was woken by my alarm. I must have reset it when I was adjusting my stop-watch. But I felt fully awake. I could just make out the white of the sheet on Mr Cool's bed, which meant it was still folded back. He'd been away for an hour.

That seemed too long to me, much too long. Unless the swine had gone fishing. My heart jumped hopefully. I dressed in the usual way and climbed out of the window. I really had no idea what I was going to do, except find a way of getting Mr Cool into trouble. The girls had said that the men were pushing their car up towards the castle. Backwards, I suppose, so that they could run it down. But why were they still here, or back here again? Why wasn't their car at the hotel, or wherever they were staying?

There were a million questions flashing about in my mind and they were driving me mad. Mad enough to forget those guys were Irish.

I began jogging towards the castle. There was no sign of the car, which meant, I guessed, that they had got it going and had gone. But where was Mr Cool? Surely goody goody Jack wouldn't have trotted off with them without permission.

Anyway, I didn't fancy going back meekly now, so I carried on.

Arriving at the castle, I found my eyes drawn to the big tower. It was a cold night, with no cloud and a lot of stars. But one was blinking. It wasn't a star, or a planet or an aeroplane. It was a different kind of blinking. I was seeing a flash of light, not the source of the light. I was seeing a torch beam that was signalling from the top of the tower.

I backed quietly into the rhododendron bushes. I wasn't sure why I should hide but it was just the way I did things. Wait, Richard, think, Richard, don't get caught, Richard.

I tried putting everything together again but it still didn't make sense.

I lit my watch. The time was exactly three fifteen. Something struck me as familiar about that time so I tried some possibilities. It wasn't sunrise – nor obviously sunset. It wasn't the time school ended, nor any of the lessons. It . . . It was high tide. I'd seen it on the board at the harbour. High tide and a full moon. Yeah.

OK. So what? Where were the Irishmen? Where was their car and where was Mr Cool? If the car was here, it must be at the far side of the castle, where I couldn't see it. But why here of all places? There was nowhere to fish from. It was miles too high and there was no way down to the sea other than the path behind our cottage, or over the rocks when the tide was lower.

My neck was prickling. I didn't like any of it now. Suppose, I thought, my heart jumping with excitement, that it wasn't one of the Irishmen up there in the tower, but instead it was Mr Cool. Mr Cool up there signalling . . . to whom . . . and why? There was nowhere to land, except perhaps the steps at the foot of the path. Mr Cool practised racing up and down those steps. Was he involved? The sneakpot! Was that why he'd tried to put me off about the map and the phone number? What was it again? 0315 13891.

That wasn't a phone number! 0315 was the time! And the other number, 13891, was the date. Yeah! I saw it now. High tide on the thirteenth of August. And there was more. The cross on the wrong tower. Why had he drawn my attention to it? Maybe Josie, and Fay even, were involved. He could have briefed them to come and get him up so he'd have an excuse.

My mind began to flood with ideas, wild but possible. The light was no longer flashing now and I could hear, in the quiet night, the footsteps of someone feeling his way down the spiral staircase.

I shrank. I reached down and spread my hands in the dirt and rubbed my face with mud. Someone came out of the door and stumbled across the ruin. He seemed to be going to the far side, presumably to where his car was parked. It didn't look like Mr Cool. The figure was clumsy and stumbling. He fell over and muttered, 'Oofya!' and swore and you could hear the Irish in the exclamation.

He emerged from the gloom and was illuminated for a moment by a shaft of moonlight, before disappearing again. Only the sound of his stumbles and then the sound of a door opening told me that the Irishman had gone to the other tower. To the one with a cross.

I waited five minutes because there was another man somewhere, besides Mr Cool, but no one came so I crossed by the shadows, towards the ruined tower. I pushed open the door and felt again a wash of cold, damp air, this time with a smell of salt and seaweed. That should have been a clue but I didn't twig until I found myself dangling from the door handle, my feet kicking into empty space.

Of course, I didn't utter a sound. I was too scared. Frightened to move, I thought quickly. Below me, between my legs in fact, was a shaft, the hinged wooden door of which lay back against the wall.

I felt about with one foot until I found a notch and then another and couldn't help a sigh of relief. Then I began to climb down. It was the kind of thing I'd never do if I stopped to think about it. So I didn't stop to think.

10

It was a good thing there was more light near the foot of the shaft because the floor was uneven, with occasional steps. I guessed I was almost down to sea level and moved carefully now, not knowing if a wall-like wave was about to surge towards me.

I pressed hard against the dark wall of the passage and slid millimetre by millimetre towards the source of the light. The air smelt damp and foul but as I moved down the passage, it grew fresher. Even so, I was almost caught off guard.

The sea had hollowed this enormous cave into a weird uneven cavern, which was lit in places by paraffin lamps. The ceiling varied from two to six metres and the walls were grooved in horizontal ridges that sometimes deepened and disappeared in the dark. Across and to my right was an arch that looked like another passage leading out of the cave. The floor too was ridged, like the rocks at the beach, with pools. Dividing the cave was a wide channel full of water. Something, somewhere, was dripping. Water lapped. But there was no other sound.

I was about to edge into the cave – there was a dark shadowy patch on the left behind a boulder which would hide me if I lay very low – when I caught sight of six wooden crates, piled on a table-sized rock. I wondered if it would be safe to move out and investigate. Where were the fishermen? Or smugglers as I now saw they were? Were there more than two? Plus Mr Cool?

Just then, I heard a sniff, a low-murmured voice, a higher pitched one, like that of a frightened girl, then a man's voice answered, brief and impatient.

I pushed my head round the wall, scraping my cheek against the cold gritty surface of the rock. Back to back, with handkerchiefs over their eyes, and their wrists and ankles tied, sat Mr Cool and Josie. Josie, you twit!

I dared not try to signal to them until I knew where their captors were. I squinted carefully round other corners for Fay. I had to assume she was here but it seemed odd that she wasn't with Mr Cool and Josie. I couldn't see a sign of anyone else and began to sum up my chance of reaching them and freeing them before the Irishmen came back.

But it was soon clear there was no time. I heard the sound of footsteps and lapping water and a curse as someone slipped. There was just time to dive behind that big rock from where I could see what was happening. I was pretty confident that I couldn't be seen in the shadow. All the same, I was glad I'd blackened my face.

The shorter of the two Irishmen, now wearing a

jacket and wellingtons, scrambled out of the further passage with a rope, pulling a wooden rowing boat. Two other men followed on either side of the boat.

One was the tall one with the lying eyes and the curly beard but it was the other who seemed to be the leader. I couldn't get a look at him for the other two stood between us, but I could hear.

'I didn't think we'd make it. Sure there's just enough water to turn the boat around. What took you?'

He proceeded to manoeuvre the boat through a hundred and eighty degrees so that it was facing back out of the channel.

'We were followed.'

'Followed!'

'Kids.'

'Kids!'

The man's voice was pitching higher in anger and disbelief.

'The worst!' he cried. 'Blue blazes! What've you done with them?'

The short man pulling the boat crouched to tie the rope to a metal ring while Curly pointed at Mr Cool and Josie.

The newcomer screamed, 'You fools, you incompetent fools bringing them here.'

He leapt over the crevice at the head of the channel and grabbed Shorty by the jacket and shook him.

'I didn't bring them here to be sure,' Shorty

stammered. 'I don't know how they saw us, for goodness sake! It was two o'clock in the morning. Who'd've thought they'd be about?'

Shorty was now strung up by the other man and gesticulating wildly with his hands but he looked pathetic and scared. I lay on my stomach, my head poking above the rock, ready to duck down should any of them turn round.

'Did they see you?'

'We-ell . . .'

'Did they?' he roared, reinforcing the question with a shake.

'We, er . . .' he cleared his throat.

The boss turned to Curly.

'We lost the map last week in the cottage. You know how we had to get out because of this family who come every year.' (I ducked down and squeezed my eyes shut as the boss began to pace the cave in frustration.) 'I couldn't risk anyone finding it. There'll be prints on it. They've got my prints, Finn. I couldn't risk it. It links us with this place and tonight for sure.'

'You bungling bunch of hopeless amateurs. In the name! You went to the house while they were there?'

'They don't go out much. There're two families you see. There's always someone there. We got Anna Cunnane to take us. They never suspected a thing.'

'I don't suppose you got it . . .'

'We did, ay we did now.'

'Ay and what they all got was a good look at yous.'

'There's no harm, Finn. They'd never associate us with this.'

'They will now, won't they?' he cried.

I fancied this was Mr Cool's cue for a challenge – like, 'You'll never get away with it!' or something. But he remained silent. Useless prat. I lifted my head again and saw the boss walk over to them. He bent on his haunches before Mr Cool.

'You could identify these two, couldn't you?'

'Yes,' said Mr Cool, his voice steady. One mark for not whimpering.

The boss snorted and got up and walked round to Josie.

'You could identify these two, couldn't you?'

I couldn't hear her reply but I guessed she had said no because the boss leaned into her face and yelled 'Liar!' causing her to flinch.

Mr Cool shouted, 'Leave her alone, you coward! She can't touch you and she's only twelve years old.'

OK. Good for you, take another point.

But the boss was unimpressed and returned to his mates leaving Josie sobbing and Mr Cool muttering, 'Don't let them see you're upset. They can't get away. Richard knows where to find us. Don't worry.'

I was touched by his faith. I couldn't see exactly how they were tied but they seemed to have little mobility.

The boss had now pulled on a pair of gloves and was loading the boxes into the boat.

'There's no time,' he said. 'You'll have to sort it out.'

The other two had joined him now in the loading operation. It didn't take long. They stood back. Shorty said, 'Er, Finn. Money.'

'Money! Ha! It won't do you much good if you're in prison.'

He jerked a finger over his shoulder at Mr Cool and Josie.

'If we go, you go.'

'Ay,' he snarled. 'You're cowards enough to squeal, damn you.'

'Well, what's to do?'

The boss hesitated, his back to me, looking into the boat as though it contained everything that mattered. What interested me was that this was his first sign of weakness or indecision. He pulled a balaclava from his pocket and yanked it over his head, arranging the hole over his eyes and nose.

'They could have a wee accident,' Curly tried.

'No!'

The boss swung round with surprising fury and held up a warning finger and I saw his face for the first time.

'No deaths. We don't kill kids.'

'You murderers!'

I hardly remember the next few seconds but suddenly I was on my feet, screaming, racing towards the men. It was six years ago now but I hadn't forgotten. I could never nor should ever forget.

'You killed my father!' I screamed. 'You murderers.'

I grabbed one of the lanterns and flung it at the boss. The man screamed and fell backwards into the boat, the paraffin spilling and the flare widening. Explosion followed explosion as wooden crates sprung apart and sprayed everywhere. The boss screamed and dived overboard into the water, his clothes on fire. Shorty, who'd been nearest, was flung through the air like a discarded puppet. Although furthest away when the explosions started – I don't know how, I must have turned and fled – I was thrown off my feet by the first blast of the ammunition catching fire.

By the time I had scrambled up, the Boss was floundering in the water, and Curly was scrambling towards me, slipping madly, his eyes wild, his mouth slobbering blood.

Josie was screaming so I knew she was all right.

I ran for the passage, listening for some noise from Mr Cool. Please be all right. I'm sorry. I'll be back. But all I could hear was Josie screaming and the man gasping and panting behind me.

'Hang on, Josie!' I yelled, plunging into the darkness of the passage.

I remembered the occasional steps and felt along the walls till my fingers burned. I reached the steep wall and grabbed at the hand and footholds. Curly was still in the passage. I began to climb.

'Stop, damn you, come back!'

Stupid thing to say, I thought calmly, concentrating on finding the steps I needed. For a moment I imagined the scene. Me saying, All right, why bother? It's pretty boring being chased. And the man saying, Oh. OK. That's very reasonable of you. Thanks. And handing me a bar of chocolate before . . .

'We don't kill kids!'

I heard someone crying. It must have been me. Because I was running from the dreadful sight of my father and the silence, the heat of the sun, the flashing explosion from the end of the shotgun, the birds going up and the silence, the siren and the silence, Mum screaming, 'You've killed my baby!' and the man screaming, 'We don't kill kids!' the footsteps and the silence.

It was all jumbled, all the noises, the pictures, all there but all jumbled.

We don't kill kids.

The worst lie of any.

All the time I was moving steadily up the shaft, my breath was coming in puffs. I was waiting every second for the scrambling, grunting and swearing below to turn into the grip of a hand on my ankle. Every time I came off one foot, I kicked into the air, just in case. I didn't dare look up. I told myself it was like the cliff path. One stage at a time. I could barely find enough oxygen. I sucked air in through my mouth. It was cold on my tongue and throat.

My fingers slipped from the sweat but were almost numb. Concentrate, concentrate. Don't panic. Got it right now, just keep going, stay cool, keep going.

The hand gripped my bare ankle and fastened round the bone. I screamed. I kicked. As it pulled, I looked up as if for a last sight of freedom. But the kick had achieved something. Curly had lost his balance and was slipping and bouncing back down the shaft.

Only he was dragging me with him.

I kicked and wriggled and tried to grab at one of the hand and foot holds as we slipped down but my fingers were raw. My knee hit a sharp rock. The pain hit me in the stomach. I felt sick but kept my concentration on the wall and began to brace myself for the landing.

As soon as I heard the rustle and bump of a stumble I looked down and saw in the faint light the man on his back, dazed. Behind him I could hear roaring and banging and crashing, Josie crying and Mr Cool shouting and Shorty yelling.

Now I was feeling for the hand grips and climbing again, ignoring the scrape on my knee which made me feel sick and the scrape on my tummy where my sweater had ridden up.

It doesn't matter, nothing matters.

I heard a wild yell from below.

'Get the kid! Get the kid!'

I climbed and climbed. I heard the scrabbling behind me as Curly reached for the same footholds.

Steady, steady, don't slip, go, go, go. I sobbed the words but they gave me a rhythm like a heartbeat, steady and reliable, go breath, go breath, go breath. I must. I must. It was a new mantra and a better one.

And suddenly my fingers reached earth that flattened in front of me and I hauled myself up the final steps and pulled down the lid and stood trembling on top of it.

'Ya dirty wee rascal!'

I jumped on the lid twice, then began to scramble over the rubble away from the crumbling walls that sent shadows like clutching hands as I passed.

And I began to run.

11

Dawn was still a way off and I was glad I knew the driveway so well. But within minutes, the sound of an engine could be heard and as I looked over my shoulder, the flicker of headlamps glinted through the trees.

I ducked into the bushes and lay flat on my stomach, panting and smelling the leafmould, watching as the car rumbled past, bumping over the ruts. They hadn't been pushing it to get it started, I realized now. They'd been pushing it past the cottage because of the noise. The track beyond the farm was too rough for an ordinary car. Bumping and rocking into the distance, the lights looked crazy.

The rest did me little good. My knee stiffened and I had to force myself into a jog. I wished I'd been able to see how many people had been in the car. Then I realized I hadn't taken a note of the number either.

I jogged on, feeling tired and beyond tiredness. This wasn't real. I wanted to shut it out. I knew how easy it was to shut out things, to change reality. But it was no good. You had to face the headache in the morning. I was nearly at the cottage and a feeling of safety and warmth and someone's arms to hide in began to creep into my hopes.

Then I remembered that there was no phone. I stopped. There was no point going to the cottage. I'd have to go to the village.

I wanted that shelter, that safety, so much. But it wasn't safety for Mr Cool and Josie. I allowed myself to carry on walking to the bend, from where I could see the cottage. I needed just to know that it was there, to look at the windows where Mum and Dad and Fay slept. I wondered whether to wake them, to tell them what was happening. But there wouldn't be time. I had to get to the phone, fast.

Then as I rounded the bend, I almost ran into the back of the car, waiting outside the cottage with no lights on. There was no sign of a driver.

I ducked behind a tree and watched, sure that if anyone were around they would hear my heart beating. An owl hooted. The silence was awful. For a minute, I believed the driver had climbed in my window and had killed everyone inside.

But I'd have heard. This is now, this is now, I told myself.

It seemed there was no movement, so I backed through the trees, carefully, trying not to snap any twigs. Something scurried under a bush but soon I reached the fence and set off across the grass. I knew it wasn't far but I had to force the jog. I kept to the side, as I'd been told. Mr Cunnane had been cutting the grass, for silage or whatever. The field was clear. Anyone could see me, running across the field in the moonlight. Anyone, that is, who was out at four o'clock on a Sunday morning.

The cows in the next field were my only audience and they ignored me, fortunately. A stampede was all I needed. At last I saw the farmhouse. I made it over the fence and stumbled noisily down the track towards the farm, where I put my head down and raced past, only stopping when I'd reached the parked jeep. The engine was warm. It didn't surprise me.

It was funny how it all came to you in one go. The trial run I'd almost stumbled on to the previous weekend. The safe house used as a holiday cottage so that no one would question new faces. The guns and ammunition stored on a farm, where there were so many hiding places. Delivered by Irish Mr Cunnane in his jeep at the appointed time. If I'd spoken to him more I'd have heard the accent before.

Then that collie went into action and a downstairs light snapped on and Mr Cunnane, fully dressed, flung open his door and called, 'What's all the racket? Sure and you're making a fine noise for four o'clock in the morning. What is it that's wrong?'

It wasn't me he was expecting to see. I ducked behind the jeep and hoped he wouldn't bother but just then the car raced up the track and stopped at the house and I heard the door open and someone shout, 'The boy's escaped! Come on!' The dog was on a chain but it was going wild and going to give me away soon, so I edged out and began to run again. This time down the farm driveway to the main road and the village. They'd need time to turn the car round. That would give me a start.

The driveway was fenced on both sides, so I ran along trying to decide which side to climb when they caught me. Half thankful for the full moon which let me see where I was going and half scared by it because it let me be seen, I stumbled on, my lungs aching.

I just ran when I could and stumbled when I couldn't. I reached the gate and shut it behind me, hoping it would delay them more than me. Then I turned right and made for the village.

The telephone box, I remembered, was in the village square. Thank goodness it was all downhill from here. I crossed the road and kept running. Part of me wondered how Mr Cool would have made out, pacing himself, sprinting, or whatever he ought to be doing. Was there some kind of training that you could do for escaping from criminals?

I reached the thirty miles an hour sign and the one that said Welcome to Greenwalls. And then I heard a car racing along the road. It was bound to be them. I stopped and gazed around for somewhere to hide but there were thick, high hedges along the side of the road. I figured they'd be looking for someone running and my only hope was to get down under the hedge. I threw myself to the ground and squeezed in as tightly as I could. I cried with relief when the car went past.

But not for long. I picked myself up and then heard another car. I turned to face it and wave it down. Help at last, I thought. Thank goodness! It's over, just about, for me. I'm safe.

It was the headlights that stopped me from recognizing it.

The jeep braked to a screeching halt. I stood there for a second, not wanting to believe what I was seeing and then I was running again, sobbing, but still running. I could never outrun a jeep. But I had to.

I found a lane that wove down hill and then up hill. After he had backed up and followed me down the narrow opening, the bends forced Mr Cunnane to go slowly and for a time it seemed that, absurdly, I could stay in front of him. I reached the square ahead. But not soon enough. The jeep was within seconds of coming round the corner. I ducked inside the bus shelter, a wooden building with a dark corner where I hoped I could hide.

The jeep slowed and circled the grassy area with its neat flower borders. While it was at the far end of the square, I sneaked clear and ran for a narrow lane that led down to the harbour. There were steps at the foot so the jeep couldn't follow.

At the harbour, I remembered that there was

an emergency phone at the hut. With a glance over my shoulder, I tiptoed across the open surface, realizing that now it was almost light, I could hardly survive by seeking dark corners. I thought I was all right for a couple of minutes anyway. I heard and saw nothing – until a hand clamped on my shoulder.

I squirmed and kicked but was grabbed from behind with my face pushed against the wall of the hut and my arms pinned behind my back.

'So you're the vandal who's been defacing our shelter, eh? Come from the city, eh? Want to turn our village into a slum so's you'll feel at home, eh?'

I remembered, in the scuffle, a navy jacket with shiny buttons, heavy creased trousers and polished black shoes.

'You're police!' I gasped.

'Ay that I am!'

'Thank goodness. Got to help me.'

'Ha! Well you're right there. I am helping you, son. Now just let's get in the car —'

'Are you on your own?'

'Think you can get away?'

'I don't want to get away.'

'Just as well.'

The grip loosened but left me in no doubt that it could be applied again immediately.

'Please sir,' I said – I had never called anyone sir before but it seemed it might help until we got the misunderstanding sorted out – 'Something very serious is happening at the castle. Smuggling.

And my cousins are hostages. We've got to get help fast.'

The policeman's face twitched.

'You've got to believe me!'

'First things first. There's the small issue of vandalism to consider. Petty I accept, not as exciting as smuggling, but . . .'

'But I haven't done anything. I'm trying to get to a phone, to phone the police for help.'

'Well.'

'What am I supposed to have done?'

'Just take a look —'

I looked at the shelter and at the painted swear-words and suggestions.

'I have no paint. I haven't done anything. You can't prove it.'

The policeman frowned.

'I can see that you don't have anything with you right now. Why were you looking so furtive as you came across the pier there? What are you doing out at this time of night?'

'I was scared. I've been chased all the way from the castle.'

At last the policeman seemed to be taking in the mud and scratches that covered me and my torn jeans and sweater. Then we were both startled by the screech of brakes.

It was the jeep.

'You'd better believe everything he says, officer,' this lady shouted, jumping out of the vehicle. 'Richard, are you all right?'

I kept the policeman between us and said, 'Who are you?'

The woman closed her eyes and swallowed. 'Yes, I can see that you're all right. Thank the Lord! I'm Mrs Cunnane,' she explained. 'When I heard Pat bellowing I was scared for you. I just ran out.'

She half smiled and opened her coat. I got a glimpse of a nightdress before she closed it again. 'Oh, thank the Lord they didn't see you!'

'It's her – her husband,' I cried. 'They carry the stuff in that jeep to the cave. That jeep's evidence.'

Mrs Cunnane looked at me closely.

'You saw?'

I nodded.

'Then . . . It's over. Thank God. It's over.'

She covered her face with her hands and sort of shuddered. Then she wiggled her shoulders. 'My son,' she said.

I hadn't time to think which one might be her son, nor did I want to.

'All right. Come and sit in the car.'

We followed the policeman to the side street where his car was parked. I sat in the back with Mrs Cunnane while he radioed my story to his central command and she tried to explain how her son had got mixed up in it and once you were in you couldn't get out even if you wanted to. The whole family were threatened if they didn't co-operate.

'Your name, son?' the policeman asked.

'Richard King.'

'Address?'

'We're staying at Greenwalls Cottage.'

'Age?'

'Fourteen. Please hurry.'

'It's all right. There's a car and an ambulance on its way to the castle right now and the coast-guard will be on their way too.'

I found myself crying and Mrs Cunnane holding me and rocking me like a baby. She was crying too.

This time, I had most of the answers the police wanted. Josie and Mr Cool were all right and they let us go home to sleep. We slept till three o'clock. It was a smashing day and all anyone wanted to do was laze about on the beach.

'Was that really the man who killed your father?' Mr Cool asked, passing me a can of coke.

'I couldn't swear to it. I mean, no, of course not. It'd be too much of a coincidence.'

'But you said —'

'It was that bit about not killing kids. That's what the, the terrorist said when he shot my father, and the rest of us. It reminded me. Made me think he was from the same crowd. That's possible.'

'And now you've stopped them.'

I looked at Mr Cool in amazement.

'Stopped them? Stopped one tiny racket. The problem's still there.'

'The political thing, you mean.'

I thought for a moment.

'Yes, there's that,' I said. 'But a political solution worked out by politicians isn't enough. It's how people feel about themselves that matters. That's what makes people do things, how they feel, not what they think. Mostly.'

'And how do you feel? Now?'

I felt as if I'd redeemed myself in Fay's eyes.

'I keep wondering if there was some way of freeing you before I got away.'

'No way, man. If you'd come anywhere near us, that great oaf would have cut off our escape. The worst part of it was that we couldn't see what was happening. We heard the explosions and the screaming and the fire but we had no idea if we'd be all right. I mean, I was hit by that piece of wood and I didn't know what else was coming. If I could've seen, I'd have known that the fire couldn't last long and couldn't spread across the rock and water.'

'That must have been scary.'

'Not half as scary as being chased.'

I helped myself to a packet of cheese and onion crisps and shifted position as I felt one side getting a bit burnt.

'Glad you could run,' Mr Cool said, with a sideways glance that admitted just a hint of admiration. 'I can't believe you don't train.'

'Well I don't. Because of all the mixed-up schooling I've had I'm behind in my lessons and I get extra English instead of sports.'

'But that's criminal!'

'Not quite. I have to get PE – it's the law – but not extra. I suppose it's right.'

'Well you get yourself caught up fast, my friend, because you've got a future in running.'

'I'm trying,' I said with an expression of mock impatience.

'What are you making faces at?' asked Dad, who'd arrived with second helpings of snack lunch.

'I'm trying to read and he keeps interrupting me.'

Dad laughed.

'He's trying to read and Jack keeps stopping him,' he repeated to everyone else.

Mum grinned.

'Well it's a much safer pastime than anything else you've been doing recently,' remarked Mum.

'Quite!' exclaimed Auntie Chris, now wearing a bright pink T-shirt with numbers all over it. 'What with his midnight feasts and Jack's midnight wanderings, I don't know! Boys!'